ROGER PULVERS is an author, playwright, theater director, translator and filmmaker. He has published more than fifty books in Japanese and English, including novels, essays, plays and poetry. Working as assistant to director Nagisa Oshima on *Merry Christmas, Mr. Lawrence* brought him back to Japan and inspired him to become the award-winning playwright, film director and prolific author he is today. His novel, *Hoshizuna Monogatari (Star Sand)*, which he wrote in Japanese, was published by Kodansha, Japan's largest publisher, in 2015, and subsequently in English and French in 2016 and 2017 respectively. It was released as a film, directed by him, in 2017. His most recent books are a novel, *Half of Each Other*, and his autobiography, *The Unmaking of an American*, both published by Balestier Press.

ALSO BY ROGER PULVERS

Half of Each Other
The Dream of Lafcadio Hearn
Liv
The Honey and the Fires
The Unmaking of an American

ROGER PULVERS

Peaceful Circumstances

A Novel

Balestier Press
London · Singapore

Balestier Press
Centurion House, London TW18 4AX
www.balestier.com

Peaceful Circumstances

First published by Balestier Press in 2019

A CIP catalogue record for this book
is available from the British Library.

ISBN 978 1 911221 46 3

Cover illustration by Lucy Pulvers

Peaceful Circumstances

It's your blueberry girl, daddy, as beautiful and innocent as I ever was. I'm here with you and I'm going to be here for you until the end.

Daddy, I was afraid you would die. I was afraid of you for as long as I can remember, but I know it isn't as long as you can remember. I've missed not being able to talk to you, like, for my whole life. Well now I can and I will, daddy. I *will*.

I'm going to sit up with you here all night. Then, in the morning, Dr. Cohen will saunter in wearing his three-piece Brooks Bros. suit with the silk polka dot handkerchief folded into a peak in his neat breast pocket. He'll stand above you, nod knowingly once or twice, cock his head to one side, pass on a few comforting words and dash out.

He won't be able to do anything for you, daddy, because, you see, you're as good as dead already. But we remember Aunt Till, don't we? Remember Till? She was dead to the world just like you are now. The doctors and nurses and even you and mom and me, when I was seven, hovered around her bed chatting away about her and Ike and everything, and everybody assumed that she couldn't hear a thing. But then one day she woke up and repeated everything to you, everything she heard said at her bedside, especially how one of the nurses had remarked on how amazing it was that she was a "big fat lump" despite being in a coma for months and being fed through the nose.

So I'm going to assume that you can hear me too, daddy, and that if you wake up you'll be able to recall everything I'm going to say to you, word for word. Didn't you once have a photographic memory? Didn't your fourth grade teacher, Miss Lyneham, praise you in front of the class for reciting the names of the leaders of the Green Mountain Boys in alphabetical order? What an achievement. I bet Miss Lyneham never forgot you, daddy.

Don't worry about a thing because I've come to look after

you tonight. I'm here to do good … to do what's right. That's what you always said to me, isn't it? "Just do what's right." Well now, finally, I'm going to do that for you. "What's right is right and there's no two ways about it." That's what you told me and it sunk in. It sunk in deep, daddy, I promise you that. That's the reason I've come back here … to do what's right by you.

"Dead from the neck up." There's another of your favorite little expressions that I have taken to heart. If Jeff couldn't get things "through his thick skull," that's what you said to him, then he was dead from the neck up. Jeff the beatnik, Jeff the no-hoper, Jeff the total loser, that's what you called your only son and heir. But heir to what, daddy? To Jeff, everything was dullsville and heavy, even your money. All that money … heavy, man, heavy. Stocks, bonds, "units" … heavy, heavy. Every question got the same answer. How was school? Heavy. How're you feeling? Heavy. His vocabulary was pretty limited, but it was expressive, don't you think? I mean, he got his point across, didn't he, your Bosco boy, your Buster Brown shoe boy, your little loser son, "slipped off the rails," as you put it. Yeah sure, he had slipped off the rails all right. Your rails. Well, he doesn't need those rails anymore. He didn't want to go on the straight and narrow. He didn't even want to move forward. But he made it, daddy, he arrived and you should be proud of him. And let me tell you, your Jeff came up in the world, way up, all the way up to Kathmandu. He had a beard longer than the tail on a donkey. I saw it in a snap he sent me. No longer your dropout trinity boy barfing over Daddy-o, J.C. and the Spook, your little queebie became a "Boodist," daddy, a dyed-in-the-wool born-again "Boodist" who wrote on the back of the snap, "Me in this life." I know he'd like to be here beside you tonight, but he won't be coming. No. He had his life to lead and there was no shifting him away from it. One clock stops and another goes on.

So, rest assured, you're going to hear everything your little blueberry girl's been doing this past year. We've got all night, so I won't be sparing you the details. You'll love the details, daddy. Isn't that where the devil is? Or was it God? You tell me, daddy. What's the difference? YOU TELL ME!

Nine months have passed since you refused to see me off and it's been a big nine months for me, one hell of a span of time, in fact. For you too, daddy. After all, you were yourself nine months ago and now you're only a blip on a screen, a shadow on a sheet. You remember your Latin, don't you, daddy? You quoted it enough times to me. You shoved Latin down my throat at dinnertime. At least we had togetherness in a dead language. *Pulvis et umbra sumus* ... We are just a shadow and dust. In reality the shadow comes first so I'm putting it first. Misquoting you back to yourself, that's what you always said I did. If I didn't agree with you, I was being "technical." But don't fret like you used to, daddy. Just don't! Don't try to bring things back. It isn't becoming of a father to bring things back, to throw things in the face of your child. And as for the dust, well, everybody else dies, so why not you? Think of yourself trapped in quicksand, like when Abbott and Costello were in the jungle. Okay, so you can't get out of quicksand by pulling on your own hair. That's a given. But it doesn't mean you can't float or tread for some time still. You're still alive, daddy, you're still with us, just like Jeff was still with us though even then he was no doubt already contemplating life as an ant or a mayfly or a dung beetle. You're lucky though because you don't have to come back. You can just go straight up ... up up and away, like the man in the beautiful balloon. So rejoice, daddy! You may be unable to move. You may be stinking with self-pity, for all I know. You may be "pretty much a hopeless case," as Dr. Cohen inelegantly put it. But at least you're a man who knows himself, a man who once had his world in the palm of his hand. So kick, daddy, kick! You can do it. A man can do whatever his heart desires, isn't that what you once said? Show some life, will you? Give me a sign that you can hear, that you are aware of these white surroundings, that you know it's me here and now talking to you. Move your index finger from side to side. Try and blink. Bare some upper teeth between your lips and bite down hard. That's not too much to ask of a man like you, is it? You're your own man, after all, aren't you? Heck, you used to be. That's what mom said of you. "Your father's his own man," she said, "his own man." But, you know, I never knew what she meant by that. Even when I asked her, she just said, "You'll understand it when you grow up." Mom aimed to please. She was eager-beaver submissive, putty in your fists. You said dive and she said to the bottom. Well you can congratulate me because I've finally grown up and I now understand what she meant by your being your own man. I read you now, daddy, loud and clear. I understand you. You *are* your own man and no one else's, there's no two ways about that. So, come on, give us a little sign … you can do it. Wag that digit. Pretend you're itching to pull a trigger. If not for yourself, pull it for our boys in the field far away from home. Our boys need you, daddy. They need you to show some life, to give them the courage to go on. They're all cut up in a boobytrapped world. They're suffering, daddy, from bamboo slivers in the soles of their feet. They're shrivelling away, daddy, they're gasping for breath, they're bleeding to death from the groin up. Our boys need you now more than you can imagine.

You're not suffering, though, thank God. You are peaceful and at rest inside your bulky shadow. You're not straying beyond its borders, not budging over the line. You know your place, don't you, daddy, and you always have. You've always been a man who has known his place. You never crossed lines. Now you've found yourself here in this white world flat on your back and as still as a marble slab. You may not be happy, but you've accepted your fate, haven't you? You must have known that it would come to this, that you'd be reduced to an outline on a sheet. You've got your catheter and your nasogastric tube. You've got your saline solution running through your veins. What more do you need now? Nothing. You've got it all, daddy.

The nurse will be in soon. She'll check the tubes once more tonight. I know what she'll say. "He seems to be resting peacefully." That's what they always say. Then she and I will have a chat about things like the weather, the episodes of Hawaii Five-O that I missed by being away and the short intern with the long sideburns. After she leaves I'll be here by your side to make sure your tubes are doing their work, that they don't slip out of their little slits. Even a man trapped in quicksand, a man who can't lift a finger or blink an eye or bare his teeth, even such a hopeless case of a man deserves to have things pumped into him and drained out of him. Yep, you're resting peacefully, and as God is my witness I'm not going to leave you now. Ever.

I saw your Dr. Rush. Nice man, Dr. Ben. That's what he said, "Call me that. Call me Dr. Ben." Nice wife. Nice kids, I mean, two nice daughters, both pretty, both blond and naturally curly. Jesus, he's got it made, that doctor. He told me to be sure to remember him to you, said you were his "mentor" at med school, said there was nothing you wouldn't do for him, said you taught him everything he knows, said he worshipped the dirt you walk over and still does. "Your dad's the greatest man I have ever known. He's a downright saint, he is. They don't make them like that anymore." Well, let me tell you that your devoted disciple is in good shape and doing a wonderful job out there for our boys, sewing them up handsomely as they make their way back from Vietnam, some of them in black bags, but others hopping. Just a little stopover in Japan to get the slivers out of their soles and the bullets out of their brains and before you know it they're heading on home for that grand train ride. I can see the festooned boxcars slowly winding their way toward the old hometown and can hear the beat of the drums of the high school band marching down main street, playing out of tune solemnly but full of heart, and I can see the girls all starched up in white with braids dripping over their golden shoulders, twirling those batons for all they're worth. They're all sayin', "Now your home, boy. Home for good."

Now, before I get too excited talking about grand homecomings, my own included, I must tell you about Eric and Hiro. You'll love to hear about them, I swear. They're … sorry, daddy, nurse's here.

—Has he been resting peacefully? I apologize for not having been in earlier. Hell of a night. Just one hell of a night.

—Yes. He's been breathing regularly. There seems to be no change.

—The cannulae seem to be fine, so I'll just empty the urine for you.

She came into the room, but has gone out now for a moment with your pee, daddy. She even shook her head to show how impressed she was with its clarity. "Good clear urine still coming out of there," she said. Good job, daddy! You're fine, aren't you, just fine, really. Temporarily laid up, that's all. And what a nurse, daddy! Nurse Arden, you'd love her, love her to bits with her big plastic name badge pinned on her left tit. She's like the milk, daddy, Arden Milk, the one that comes in the big carton. Oh, I wish you could've seen her holding that sleek yellow bottle in her warm little hands. You would've sat up in bed, smiled and said, "You are so kind to an old man like me." But even if you missed the sight, you did at least hear her voice, didn't you? Think of it, cannulae … getting the Latin plural right! How many people could do that nowadays? You can't tell these days, can you, about people. Some of them are still as good as people used to be. Nurse Arden, daddy, Nurse Arden! She's here again, she's here, and she's bending over you, way down low.

—I'll just attach this back on, and Bob's your uncle.

—Thank you. And I thank you on behalf of my father.

—What a kind and sweet young woman you are! I wish all young women were like you. Sadly, they're not. You see a lot of the other sort here. They sit down with their scuzzy little miniskirts hiked right up to north of the border. Some of them have these beads, their hair looks like a Mexican breakfast, and they chew gum like cud and can't wait to get out of here. "How much longer?" they ask. And I can tell by their tone of voice that all they want is for it to be over soon, to get their old parent or grandparent or aunt or uncle out of their kinky hair. But you're different. You're just like Margie Albright? She took care of her father. You're the best.

—Sorry, who?

—Oh, I guess you're too young for that. Mother not coming in? You'd expect …

—She's dead. She died of cancer of the ovaries in this hospital. Two years ago.

—Oh my gosh, you've had that too. I wasn't here then. I was still over in Vegas then. Decided I'd had it. Not the place it used to be. Used to be a family place. Even the shows have changed. The magic's gone, know what I mean? The magic's gone out of the whole damn country, if you ask me. No, you are the best. I can tell about young women when I see them, right when I set eyes on them. Well, I'm going off now. There's no nurse on tonight, but Dr. Price's around.

—Dr. Price?

—Uh-huh. The intern, you know, the one with the sideburns. Looks a bit like Sal Mineo, don't you think? Too young for me, though. He calls me "matron." Fancy that.

(Oh, she's adjusting her bosom, daddy!)

—I guess so.

—Guess what?

—He looks like Sal Mineo. I mean, the type.

—Short but, you know, kind of, I mean, swarthy and, um, stocky. I like a man with meat on him. He's around if you need him.

—I'll be all right. We'll be all right.

—Sure. Anyways, Dr. Cohen'll be in in the morning, first thing, like he said. He'll fix up the drip and things.

—We'll be fine. Thank you.

—Sure. If you notice him having trouble with his breathing, though, just press the call button. I'll alert Dr. Price to listen for the buzz. Just in case. He'll be here for you all night. Call him in. They stop breathing, that's what we've got to worry about.

—I'll be sure to press the button if there's a problem.

—Good night, then. Um, what was it?

—Sorry?

—Sorry, your name. I didn't get your name.

—Karen.

—Karen, I'm Kathy. Kath Arden. Well, um, goodnight, Karen. I'm bushed. I wish everybody was as good as your father. He's a lucky man.

—Yeah, that's right. Good night.

She's gone now, daddy, Nurse Arden, and we're alone again, just you and me. Shame you didn't get a good look at her when she bent over your bed. Anyway, you've got your tubes and you've got me here to keep you alive. You've got me all night long. I'm going to tell you everything. You're going to hear it too. I know you are. I'm not going to let you get away, no siree Bob. You're going to listen, daddy. For once in your life, you're going to listen to ME.

Jeanette is almost exactly a year younger than me, though she acts a lot older, if older just means putting on gobs of makeup and talking about things like your breasts. But you would know all about that, wouldn't you, daddy? I would walk into her room, which was across the hall from mine, and there would be fourteen colored bras on the bed lined up like lollipops. She stands over them like women do in the frozen meat section at Ralphs, with her chin resting on her knuckles like the statue of that guy by the French sculptor, the guy who's really steeped in thought. She's standing in her nightgown just gazing down at her bras like she's contemplating the biggest decision in her life. Fran, who's the daughter you never met, is only thirteen and a half but she thinks her sister's goofy, going ape over something like a bra. Ben and Ethel don't have a clue about what goes on in the girls' bedrooms. They leave the girls to their own devices. Not like you, daddy. You turned all the knobs, you held on to all the controls, you gripped them tightly, you never let go, did you, daddy.

Mrs. Duvall, that's Ethel's mother, arrived on a Pan Am jet in a wheelchair because she had had a stroke just like you, though she was quite jolly. I went to Haneda Airport with Ethel to help get her, even though I had arrived in Tokyo myself only a couple of days before. She drooled a lot and couldn't speak clearly and did everything with her left hand but she said she met you once when you gave a speech at Ben and Ethel's wedding. But then she had another stroke in the middle of October and Ethel took her back to L.A. and stayed there for about a month. The whole house in Tokyo fell to pieces and Jeanette sort of freaked out. Even though Ethel came right back, by Christmas the Rush home had become a warzone and I'm going to tell you about it when I think you're ready to hear it.

Ben made sure though that Ethel was in the Tokyo house well in time for Thanksgiving, which was just before I moved out. Yes, daddy, I moved out. But I know what happened in the Rush household after that because Jeanette kept me informed.

Ben asked me to say the Thanksgiving prayer, but you know all too well that I'm no good at that sort of thing, so Ethel came to the rescue and talked about the Pilgrims and how much hardship and suffering they had to go through in a hostile environment, and then Ben dished out the stuffing and cranberry sauce while Fran poured much too much cold brown gravy over everybody's turkey. They didn't say much to each other during the meal except for talking about what they were going to do after Christmas, which was take a trip to Okinawa before it gets given back to the Japanese, which Ben said was "on the cards." Fran said she couldn't believe she was going to be fourteen next year, and Ben made us all pray again for peace which he was sure would come soon, and he wouldn't have to sew up all those boys anymore because "Richard Milhous Nixon was certain to be our next president and put a stop to everything."

They all asked me what my plans were after I moved off the base, after all, life at Tachikawa was just like at home, they said, and it wasn't a hostile environment like off the base could be. They could see that I wasn't about to agree with calling someone else's country a hostile environment, so Ben chuckled it off saying it was only a joke. What was bothering me though was not jokes like that but that they would say them, and much more inflammatory things, right in front of the maid Kimiko who's a Japanese after all, right to her face without blinking, as if she was a mechanical doll in a museum or something. Kimiko's seventeen, so she's really between Jeanette and Fran. She gets along with both of them. She told me she didn't mind anything because she was there to learn English not to serve American people. When Ethel and Jeanette were clearing the table Ben lectured me about the Civil War, of all things, just like you used to, though to give you your due you hopped more from one war to the next, remember? Each war contained a lesson for the next one, isn't that what you always said? "A never-ending story," that's what you called it. Ben talked about how Lincoln singlehandedly freed the slaves and what a great man and a great president and a great commander he was too, and that he was and will always be those things for as long as we live, and then Jeanette returned from the kitchen and just stared at her father with squinty eyes like he was speaking a foreign language. If I didn't know that she was his daughter I would've thought at that moment she was some kind of crazywoman who might've picked up the greasy carving knife left on the table and shoved it right through her father's heart. Then she sort of laughed it off by blowing air out of her nostrils, like, snorting, picked up the carving knife, wiped it on her clean pretty pink dress and went back into the kitchen. I didn't know what was behind the look in her eyes and the wiping of the greasy knife on her dress until Christmas, but now I wonder why she was staying at home at all. She should've left like me. But unlike me I guess she had nowhere else to go, no way to get herself out of her life up to then. It was Eric and Hiro who showed me that I could do it for good. She didn't have anybody like that, no savior.

The next morning after breakfast when Ben came in dressed in his smart uniform which they had put so much starch in at the base dry cleaners that his trousers creaked when he sat down, the Rush family got into a huge argument, worse than anything I'd seen there, and I felt so embarrassed for myself and Kimiko, although some of the fights you had with Jeff were far more scary, like two men fighting on the edge of a cliff and one is bound to fall. I stayed as quiet as I could because I had lived with them for over two months since I got to Japan and wanted to move out leaving as favorable an impression as possible.

The problem was a yellow packet of Peace cigarettes that Ethel had found in Jeanette's underwear drawer two days before, but had only told Ben about that morning when they woke up. They get everything they use at the PX like the Aunt Jemima pancake mix and the Log Cabin syrup in a can shaped like a log cabin and Ethel's Maybelline mascara stuff that she lets Jeanette use when she goes out on a date. But the PX doesn't have Japanese cigarettes only American ones, so Ben wanted to know where Jeanette got them from. I mean, it wasn't as if he was even furious about her smoking, just that he was suspicious of her getting things from someone off the base. I think Fran had caught on earlier than anyone to why her father was flipping his lid and that's why she was giggling, which Ben put a stop to by glaring at her. So Ethel intervened because she knew that otherwise there would be an atomic explosion right there in the breakfast nook and asked Jeanette in a really nice way where she got the Japanese cigarettes from. Jeanette just said, "From somebody," and Ethel asked very politely and in a soft voice who it was, but Jeanette just said one word, "Somebody." That's when Ben raised his voice a bit and said it couldn't have been an American boy because he would've given her Camels or Luckies or some other American brand, so this somebody must've been a Japanese boy and, if he was, then that would be the end once and for all of Jeanette going out at night because no daughter of his would be seeing a Japanese individual off the base. Ethel intervened again but not this time to calm things down. She said what hurt the most was that Jeanette was doing something in secret and lying. She told the two girls this, but avoided looking at me when she said it. She also said that this is the sort of thing that hurts God too. After Jeanette left the table without eating a thing or even finishing her bottle of Dr. Pepper, Ben and Ethel had a long discussion about her. Fran asked if she could visit her friend Marsha and Ethel said, "Sure," so she left right away. I finished cleaning up because Kimiko had gone to her room to listen to the radio or something. Technically she could have had Sundays off so she didn't have to do the cleaning up, and she wasn't required to go to church either because she told me she didn't believe in God, not like "you people" do. I thought it funny those two months I was with the Rushes that they would talk about absolutely anything right in front of me like I wasn't there at all. They didn't seem to be embarrassed by anything. Maybe they were treating me like another daughter, seeing as you are the girls' godfather.

Ethel came into the kitchen when I was doing the drying up to explain things to me so that I wouldn't think badly of their family. She said that Ben was naturally worried about his daughter because they want her to only go out with nice American boys. She's twenty-one and can do what she likes, she said, but that doesn't mean she can do whatever she likes. It was okay to see anyone at the N.C.O. Club for a movie or even for some jitterbugging, as she put it, but it wouldn't do to go wandering off the base like a stray dog. In the end, she said, "Tachikawa is our home base here, our home away from home." Then she asked me if I knew whether Jeanette was seeing a Japanese boy, and I told her that I had no idea and that we didn't talk about boys or that sort of thing. Ben was standing in the kitchen doorway listening to us. He finally spoke up.

—You be careful too, Karen. Girls your age are very impressionable. I could never forgive myself to your father.

So, daddy, you can see that it was very educational staying with your favorite disciple and his family. What happened after that at Christmas was a catastrophe for them, but in the end I don't want to worry you because they avoided all the consequences magnificently and that's the main thing, isn't it? Everybody has catastrophes in his life but not everybody can avoid paying the price for their consequences. The Rushes are the kind of people who don't pay. Just like you, daddy. You can do things with impunity, that's the word, isn't it? No punishment. Maybe that's why you're his great teacher, like a man who guides others through life without having to take account of his own. Remote control. You're inside Ben Rush. If anybody knows that it's you, daddy. You know how to create miracles with people from afar, don't you. You're a miracleman, daddy. You're really one of God's little miraclemen.

As I was about to tell you when Nurse Arden walked in, it wasn't long after that that I met Eric. You like that name, don't you, daddy? ERIC. Eric's a good name, a staunch name. Staunch and upright. Good man, Eric, good man. There's only one trouble with my Eric though. Eric's a Negro. Fancy that, daddy, a Negro named Eric. Bet you didn't know there were Negroes named Eric. When I wrote Jeff about it he was really impressed. He said, "That's heavy, man, heavy." Oh, how I would've liked to see you shake hands just once with Eric, daddy! He has big hands, you know, enormous hands. He would envelop your right hand until all you could see was little specks of cracked white sticking out from under black silk. I swear, I would've given a million dollars to see you two shaking. But it wasn't meant to be, was it, daddy. Things got in the way of that. They didn't have to but they just did.

I had no idea what city I was in until I left the base at

Tachikawa to live in Jinbocho. For two months my whole life had been the base except for one excursion with the Rushes to see the department stores on the Ginza. But that was the plan, wasn't it? Karen would spend her junior year abroad safely tucked away on "our" base in Tokyo, studying at the University of Maryland extension right on the base. You asked Dr. Ben to set it up, and of course nothing would make him happier than to be able to "give back" something to you, as he said to me. I would live with him, Ethel, Jeanette and Fran as a kind of third daughter and sister. I would have my fling with freedom for a year before returning to U.S.C. Then I would meet Bob or Jim or Frank or Bill, who would be a professional man, an accountant or at the very least a dentist, get married and settle down in L.A. once and for all. But I deserved to see a bit how people on the other side of the planet lived first, right?

But heck, daddy, it went haywire, real haywire. The problem was that after I left Tachikawa I saw that people lived in houses where they didn't have lawns to mow. People stood next to each other in crowds and minded their own business. And they walked! That was the thing that amazed me the most, actual people walking. I don't remember walking anywhere in L.A. I mean, who walked?

I went to my classes on the base faithfully, I promise you I did. I did my essays, the few of them I had to do. I saw a couple of movies at the N.C.O. Club. I helped around the Rush household doing more than Jeanette, although that's not saying much. But then I made one mistake, at least from your standpoint. I went by myself into the city. I didn't do it of my own accord though. It was my professor of poli sci, Prof. Cromwell, who recommended I go to a bookstore where they sell used books in English and find something on World War I with realistic photographs. The extension library on the base was "sorely lacking," Prof. Cromwell said.

So I took an excursion, a side trip, and that's what started the fall off the cliff's edge of your little blueberry girl, daddy, the precipitous fall of your pride and joy … your one and only little angel.

I was standing in the Western history section of the Miyazawa Bookstore in Jinbocho staring at an oil painting of a woman in a wedding dress soaring through a starry sky above tenement buildings in a crowded city, her neck stretched to one side and twisted upward, when he said his first words to me.
—What do you think?
I swivelled around.
—What do you think?
—Sorry?
—I was wondering what you thought of the painting.
—It's, yeah, it's, uh, good.
He nodded his head, folding his arms over his chest.
—What's good about it?
—I don't know. I don't know much about modern art really.
I turned back toward the painting. We were the only two people in the bookstore. The sun was shining through the big window that faced the main street. There was a faint smell of mold in the air.
—It's Harlem.
—Harlem? That's amazing. I did hear about that in an art history lecture. Holland was so amazing, with Rembrandt and things.
He burst into a laugh.
—Nope. Wrong Harlem. Closer to home. You're American, aren't you?
—Yes. I'm from L.A.
—Oh, that explains it. So you've at least heard of Watts?
—Sure. That's where the riots were.

—Gotta be famous for something. Harlem is the New York Watts.

—Sorry? I saw them on TV, the riots, I mean. Not that I've ever been to *that* part of town.

—*That* part of town. Well, maybe people in *that* part of town have never been to your part of town.

I stepped away from the picture and strolled along the bookshelves, pretending to be looking for a book.

—Eric's the name. Eric Smith.

He put out his hand, walking toward me, and we shook.

—Hi. I'm Karen. Karen Rogers.

—No relation to Will, I suppose.

—No, of course not. But we do live not far from the state park in his honor. I went to Pali High, then U.S.C., I mean, I'm still at U.S.C., technically.

—Now it's me who has to say sorry. What's Pali High? Sounds like a song out of "South Pacific."

—Funny you should say that because that's the school song we used to sing to the tune of "Bali Hai" but with Pali High instead. Do you know Pacific Palisades? It's really beautiful there.

—I've heard of it. Thomas Mann lived there, when he was in L.A. I do know that.

—Who?

—Look, this conversation is really not going very smoothly. It's all my fault. I should never have asked you what you thought of my painting.

—You painted that?

—Yup.

—It's beautiful.

—Now you're talking! Music to a young artist's ears. Although I haven't painted a thing since coming to Japan.

I walked along the bookshelf back to the painting.

—I really like the neck. It's like her neck is propelling her forward or upward or something.

—Look, uh, Karen, can I call you that?

—It's okay.

—This place is an awful place to talk. The air is dusty or something, I don't know. Want to have a coffee?

—I don't know. I came to …

—You can come back after. I'll help you look for your books. I know these shelves like I know my bookshelves at home. It isn't, uh, that I'm a Negro, because …

—No, of course not.

—I won't go rioting, not around here anyway.

—No, fine. I have all afternoon. Sure, why not?

Eric took me across the street and down an alley to a hole-in-the-wall coffee shop beside a bookstore with gold lettering in Russian on the window.

—I didn't mean to, I mean, make a point about Watts or anything. Really. It's not my scene, anyway.

—No, that's okay.

There were colorful rugs hanging on the walls of the coffee shop and some kind of guitar or ukelele music was coming from two speakers standing on little shelves in the far corner of the room.

—I don't know much about them really, but my dad says that Martin Luther King caused the Watts riots.

Eric burst into laughter again, this time much louder than before.

—Haven't heard that one before.

—I don't know. It's just a theory.

—How did he manage to do that, I wonder? How did Dr. King cause the riots?

—Dad says by being inciteful.

—Hmm. Is that with a "c" or an "s"?

—I don't follow.

—Never mind. Have a seat. That's the owner over there, the man behind the counter in the rubashka. That's a Russian shirt.

—Is this a Russian coffee shop?

I looked around, feeling suddenly ill at ease.

—No, it's a Japanese coffee shop, Karen. It just happens to be next to Nauka, the Russian bookstore. You look like you've seen a ghost, a communist ghost. Relax. They're not communists in here, at least I don't think they are. It's just a plain normal Japanese coffee shop, except that it's one that plays Russian balalaika music instead of American jazz or rock 'n' roll or classical music like most other Japanese coffee shops. What would you like?

—I'll have a coffee, please.

Eric called out to the manager and ordered.

—I could tell you ordered coffee. It's *ko-hi*, isn't it?

—That's right. I only know really a handful of words and expressions. So you speak Japanese, Karen?

—Just a few words too. I've only been here, like, two months, but I've had almost no contact with Japanese people except the maid at the home I'm living in.

—You're living in a home with a maid?

—Yeah, a Japanese maid.

—Must be some mighty rich people. Wow.

—I don't think so. He's a doctor. On the base.

—Base? You mean, like, army base? American army base?

—Uh-huh. Tachikawa.

—Jesus. I never would've guessed it, an army brat.

—Oh no. I'm not in the army, I mean, my dad's not in the army. It's sort of complicated, but Dr. Rush is a close friend of my dad's. So, when my junior year abroad sort of came up, dad got in touch with him and asked if I could stay.

—Not much of a junior year abroad on an army base. Pretty

much the same as staying in Pacific Palisades, I would think, except you can't see the Pacific from Tachikawa and people's lawns are smaller.

—Have you been out there?

—To Tachikawa?

—Yes.

—Nope. But I'm stationed at Camp Zama. Pretty much of a muchness.

—You mean, you're a soldier?

—Yep. Till the day I die, if not sooner.

—How come you're not wearing your uniform?

—We don't wear them when we come into the city. It incites the natives.

—Is that incites with a "c"?

—Ow, touché, you got me there.

The manager brought two cups of coffee on a tray, put them on the table, smiled, said, "Two American," bowed and walked back to the counter.

—What did he mean by that?

—American? It's what they call their bland tasteless coffee here. "American."

—Oh.

—So, what's a nice sweet American girl doing in a strange place like this?

—Tokyo?

—No. I got that already. Jinbocho, the bookstore capital of the Orient.

—Well, my poli sci professor at the University of Maryland extension on the base recommended that I get a book on World War I. There's next to nothing in the library there with pictures. I think he wanted me to get off the base, too, to see a bit of the real Japan. I was feeling a bit, uh, cloistered up.

—University of Maryland extension? Extension of war, that's

what it is. They're under contract from the Department of Defense.

—I don't follow. They're a real university.

—Sure they are. They all are.

Eric looked around the coffee shop, and I followed his eyes. There were two other young couples in the room, both Japanese. One of the couples was holding hands over the table.

—So, what else did your dad say?

—About what?

—Anything.

—He's not prejudiced, if that's what you mean. Our cleaning lady is a Negro and she's been with us since I was little, since as long as I can remember. We treat her like we would treat anyone else. Better, actually.

—Sorry. I didn't mean that. What I meant was, about your coming all by yourself to a strange country.

—Well, my brother Jeff's in Nepal, though dad really disapproves of that. Mom died, like, over a year ago now, so I guess he's feeling pretty lonely. But he's got his work. He's a doctor, a thoracic specialist. And he's really involved in politics and things. Do you know, he was even campaigning on the telephone for Richard Nixon when he was running for Congress when I was born, well around then.

—Very impressive.

—Dad says that only Nixon can win the war for us.

—Does he now.

—Uh-huh.

—And do you agree, Karen?

—I don't know. Dad is pretty sure. But we have to win. We can't lose.

—Well, we *could* lose.

—No we couldn't. America has never lost a war.

—There's always a first time.

—Not for America. How could America lose? Other countries lose. We don't. It's just not something we do.

I took a sip of coffee. Eric was staring at me, and I suddenly felt uncomfortable.

—I really like your painting, Eric.

—Thanks a lot.

—No, really. You have a lot of talent, even I can see that.

—My art appreciation teacher at Rutgers used to think so. He saw my paintings and said I was going to be the Negro Chagall.

—I don't know that artist.

—He's Jewish, from Russia. So I decided to drop out for a year, go to New York and pursue my art. The only trouble was that Uncle Sam pursued me there first and I was drafted because like an idiot I hadn't held on to my student deferment. Then they sent me here. I've haven't held a brush in my hand since. Just guns and grenades.

He stirred two sugars into his coffee and took a big drink.

—Well, it's like a junior year abroad, I guess. You might be stimulated by it, to do even better things, I mean. Every experience takes on meaning for later life. Oh golly, that was a banal thing to say.

—Stimulated, yeah. Stimulated in Vietnam. That's where we're headed, Karen. I expect to ship out next spring. That's when they expect the next big offensive from the Viet Cong to come.

—But you'll be defending our country. Somebody's got to do it or else.

—Or else what?

Eric stared at me again, holding the rim of the cup to his lips. He slowly put the cup down. The music came to an end and the manager in the Russian shirt took the record off the record player, blew on it and slipped it into its cover.

—Let's get back to the bookstore, okay? I can help you get

that book you need about World War I.

—Did I say something wrong? I think I really sounded like Billy Graham at the Coliseum.

—Of course you didn't say anything wrong, Karen. You said all the right things. Really. It's just that I'm meeting my friend Hiro at the bookstore at 12:30. He's the owner's nephew. So I'd better be getting back. The coffee's on me.

—Oh, thank you very much.

As we left the coffee shop, I glanced back from the doorway. Now both couples were holding hands. The manager was leaning against the counter listening to a choir of deep male voices singing a Russian song. Outside the door a cold wind swept dead leaves into a twisting pillar of air, and I waved my hand in front of my face to brush away the dust.

—Did you say you went to Rutgers? Oh, that's such a strong wind.

—Yeah. Don't tell me you know someone there.

—Well, Paul Robeson.

—You know Paul Robeson? What?

Eric stopped in his tracks on the sidewalk and shivered, rubbing his arms.

—Of course I don't. But I know he went there because he talked about it when I heard him sing "Ol' Man River" once at the Hollywood Bowl. My friend Carole took me there, well, her dad did. He was a colleague of my dad's.

—You saw Paul Robeson sing? That's really outta sight. Can I touch you?

—Well, Eric, I may not be as naïve as I look, you know.

He gently put his hand against my back as we stepped off the curb and crossed the street.

I know that I said I would go into all the details, daddy, but there really isn't much more to tell about that first meeting.

Eric's friend, Hiro, was waiting for him at the bookstore. I think he was surprised to see Eric walk in beside a blond white girl.

It was funny at first to see them together. Eric towered a good head and shoulders over Hiro, but anybody could see from the outset that they were close friends. They talked in English almost like brothers, interrupting each other, laughing, sort of horsing around by patting each other on the shoulder, though Hiro had to raise up his arm to pat someone so much taller than he was. I learned the Japanese word for Negro, too, daddy. It's *kokujin* … "black person."

Eric asked if he could have my telephone number and I gave him the Rushes' number because that's the only one he could reach me on. I wouldn't have given it to him, but he's really very nice and a lot better educated about the world than I am. I never had a Negro friend or even an Oriental one, and Carole was my only Jewish friend at Pali High.

That's all it was in the very beginning, daddy, so don't fret. It was nothing more than that, except for Eric's taking the time to find me a book with photographs of World War I battlefields in Belgium and France and countries like that. They've got these gorgeous poppies growing all over them and long kind of billowy grass and lots of shrubs, and it all looks so peaceful, daddy, really peaceful even though there are tens of thousands of bodies buried under there. I skipped lunch and got back to home base before three. No one but Kimiko was home and I told her everything, just like I'm telling you now.

I couldn't get into my studies after that. Somehow they seemed so detached from the real world. Oh, the facts were okay. But the way my professors spoke about them, even Prof. Cromwell, no especially Prof. Cromwell, it was as if everything that ever happened from ancient Greece and Rome right up to the present was leading up to things America had to do. When I showed him the book of photographs he got all teary and said, "We should have put a stop to it." When I asked him what it was that we should have put a stop to, he stared into the distance. "It's all about the triumph of good over evil," he said. "That's what it's always about, Karen."

It was around the end of the first week in December when I started skipping classes. Sometimes Ethel was home, so I couldn't very well go back there. It was all right when only Kimiko was home because she knew I didn't really have my heart in my studies anymore. So I took to going into the city and exploring places like Shinjuku and Shibuya and the Meiji Shrine and even as far away as Ryogoku by the Sumida River where I saw my first sumo wrestler who would've even made Eric look like a weedy little kid. When I got home from the city one day Ethel asked me where I had been and for the first time I lied to her and told her I was in class. I think she suspected that I hadn't been there by the way she squinted at me. For one thing my duffel coat and clothes were sort of different from the ones I wore to class, which was just a couple of blocks away on the base. But she didn't say anything. Then the phone rang and Kimiko answered it like she always does.

—Rush residence. Yes, one moment please. It's for you, Karen.

Ethel was surprised because it was the first phone call I had gotten there except for when you called the day after I arrived, daddy, to make sure I was safe.

—Who was it, Karen?

—Just a guy.

—A guy?

—Uh-huh. A guy named, uh, Eric, Mrs. Rush.

—Oh. A fellow student?

—Uh, he's a soldier, yeah.

—Oh, that's nice. Ask him around sometime. We'd love to meet him.

—Okay. Sounds good. Uh, Mrs. Rush?

—Yes.

—He's, uh, Eric's asked me to go on a date. But he knows I have to be home by ten and he'll make sure I get safely to the gate.

—Well, that sort of thing is up to you, honey. Your father trusts you, as we do. We might know Eric. What's his last name?

—Oh, he's not here at Tachikawa. He's at Camp Zama.

—Camp Zama? That's a long way away. You sure he can get you back here on time?

—Oh, absolutely.

—Where are you going, may I ask?

—Uh, we're meeting at Jinbocho.

—Where's that?

—It's in the city. It's where all the bookstores are.

—Sounds very educational. Just kidding, honey. You go out and have a good time. When is it? It's not on Sunday, is it?

—No, tomorrow, Saturday. We're meeting at five.

I didn't tell her that Eric was taking me to Roppongi, to a nightclub. It would only disturb her, and Dr. Ben would never approve. But I had to tell somebody because I had never been to a nightclub before, so I told Fran who said it was so bitchin'. I swore her to secrecy because if Jeanette found out she would find a way to use it against me, if only to protect herself from her father.

I told Eric everything, daddy, except for that one big thing that's our little secret. I told him about how we saw Leo Carrillo leading the Rose Parade on his white horse, how the Edgemar milkman sat me on his lap and took me for a spin around Crenshaw Village in his truck and about when Sam Yorty came to our house asking for your support in his campaign to be mayor and when a long time before that Mr. Hearst patted me on the top of the head though I really wouldn't have remembered that if you hadn't told me, and you said he was going to change the name of Westlake Park to MacArthur Park after the general, and we went boating at night on the glassy surface of the lake there and Jeff put his head in his hands when he saw the reflection of the yellow lights on it and screamed, "Daddy, daddy, look, there are stars twinkling in the water!" Eric said it sounded just so "all-American" and I asked him what he meant. I mean, it's not as if Eric didn't grow up pretty much just like me, and it wasn't in Harlem or anywhere else like that. He grew up in Orange, New Jersey, best food, best education, holidays in Europe as a kid with his parents and big brother, Gordon. His dad owns a chain of hardware stores and his brother Gordon stayed on to help run them instead of going to university like Eric. One day a white protection gang, some members of it, came into the head store and Gordon refused to pay and threatened to notify the police, so they beat the living daylights out of him and broke both his arms and said that if he didn't come up with the money by the next day they'd break his neck too. So Eric's parents sent Gordon to Canada. But when he came back nine months later to go to his mom's funeral who died from lung cancer because she was a heavy smoker, the gang members were waiting for him at the graveyard. Apparently they saw the funeral notice in the paper and figured he might be there and they carted him away with a gun between his ribs and that's all Eric or his father ever saw of Gordon again. So Eric has a real cause for having a grudge against white people, but he doesn't at all and he said, "Well, I guess my upbringing was very American too, Karen, just like yours."

Eric and I met up with Hiro and his girlfriend Emi in front of the Almond coffee shop in Roppongi. It was my first time in

Tokyo at night and I'd never seen anything like it. The freeway runs right overhead and there are even more people milling about everywhere than around Clifton's Cafeteria or when we went to Grauman's Chinese for that Elks Club special preview of "The Ten Commandments." A few blocks down and around the corner from Almond we went into this nightclub on the fourth floor and there were a lot of Americans, about half white and half Negroes and the rest Japanese, girls too. Eric asked if I wanted to drink and I said something soft, but Hiro recommended the maitais there and that's what we all had. Mine and Emi's came with a little pink paper Japanese umbrella sticking up out of it. I decided to drink it but real slowly, and we watched the couples dancing to music played by a Japanese jazz band.

—You're a bit of an enigma, Karen, you know that?

—Why?

He really took me aback with that.

—Well, I mean, seeing you here, just sitting here, uh, completely unfazed.

—What do you mean? Why should I be fazed? You brought me here.

—I mean, doesn't it strike you yourself as, sort of, I mean, incongruous, if you could see yourself here in this club? Those guys are soldiers who are fed up to the back teeth with what America's doing and by all rights you are, I mean, sort of a fish out of water here, aren't you? And yet you don't seem, well, flustered or anything.

—I believe in freedom, if that's what you mean. Everybody has a right to his own opinion. Whatever those guys think that's their business so long as they don't push it onto other people.

Eric laughed deep down in his throat and slapped his palms against the table. Neither Eric nor Hiro said anything, they just exchanged a glance. It was Emi who spoke next.

—Freedom to kill innocent Vietnamese people. Is that

freedom too?

Eric could see that Emi's comment had bothered me.

—Come on, let's dance.

He stood up, offering me his hand. The band was just starting to play "The House of the Rising Sun." Eric wasn't a very good dancer, daddy. See? You can't judge every book by its cover, like you once said. If you were conscious I'd expect you to say, "I bet he was a good dancer." When we were dancing he whispered into my ear.

—I love the Animals.

—Which animals?

—Oh my, Karen, you are an enigma, man, one big hell of an all-American enigma.

—I know which Animals, Eric. Can't you tell when someone's pulling your leg?

He drew his chin in and stared at me.

—Wow. I'm gonna have to keep an eye on you.

I felt strongly that Emi hated me from the beginning, but it wasn't as if I was the one killing innocent Vietnamese people. It was the soldiers like some of the ones in that club who would be sent there before long. The band had stopped playing and we were standing on the dance floor waiting for the next song.

—But there is a choice that they, I mean, people, Americans, you know, have.

—What choice, Eric?

—Not to go. That's the choice. Not to make the soldiers go.

—But it's your duty. You've got to have duty if you're going to have a country.

—Duty? I have a duty to kill innocent people? Is that what you're telling me? Is that what you're telling these guys here, your only choice is to murder innocent people? For what? Can you tell me that? So that they can live with the memory of it for the rest of their lives? Is that their duty?

—It's your, I mean, well, your mission.

—Ah, mission! And who're the missionaries, eh? Don't tell me you're one of the missionaries.

We sat back down at the table.

—What are you so angry about, Eric? We're a democracy. If people didn't want you to go on their missions for them, they wouldn't send you.

—People, is it? Look around this room, Karen. More than half of the guys here are Negroes. Why is it that they're the ones who're going to Vietnam, so many of them, eh?

Hiro nodded.

—And the Japanese people. They give all their support and money to America.

—I didn't send you to Japan, Eric.

—Who did, your wonderful old Nixon-loving daddy?

—Don't you bring my father into this. It's so unfair. You don't know him, you don't know him at all.

—Sorry. But look around you. What's fair about this? These guys are just like me and we're being turned into murderers so that Americans in L.A. and Iowa and Kansas and New Jersey can be free? Free from what? Give me a break, Karen.

Emi stood up abruptly.

—I don't want to stay here any longer.

I could see by the way she was avoiding looking at me that I was the reason why she wanted to leave. We all decided to go, and we walked out together, parting when we were back in front of Almond. It was already approaching nine and there were even bigger crowds of people milling on the streets than before.

—I'll take you back to Tachikawa now.

—No, that's fine, Eric. I can make my own way.

—Really?

—I'm fine, really. I'll go home by myself.

—I think I was really rude to you back there. I'm sorry. I have no right to talk to you that way. It's just something that's really getting to me, that's all. I have to live with it every day. Look, I'll take you as far as Shinjuku. Let's take a cab. I've got money to burn.

—You don't think much of me, do you. You think I'm an apologist, right?

—What?!

He took my hand in his and held it to his chest. He hailed a cab with his free hand and we jumped into the back seat.

—Listen. You're not the first white girl I've been out with. Gordon was going to get married to his girlfriend Luisa, she was Italian-American. I don't understand you, Karen. I don't know, maybe I just see something in you. Maybe I want to be there when it comes out from under your skin.

That was when Eric kissed me, daddy, not on the lips but once behind my ear. He whispered "Sorry" to me again and we rode pretty much in silence all the way to Shinjuku. He was still holding my hand in his. More than the conversation at the club, more than that cab ride with the nighttime lights rushing past us like a kaleidoscope, more than Eric's hand over mine like a soft glove or his kissing me, more than anything, daddy, it was those words that became the impetus … "maybe I just see something in you." What on earth did Eric see in me? That was the thing I wanted to find out most.

It was just before eleven when I reached home. Jeanette was still up. She had been on a date too, at the N.C.O. Club with John.

—Do you like him?

—John? Not really, Karen. He's really sweet and polite-like and then he gets completely out of hand. He's always asking me my opinion of things, I mean, songs and movies and things.

He seems to really care. I like that. The other guys I've gone out with are all just interested in one thing. John's interested in that too, I mean, but he doesn't have a one-track mind and I ... I ... I mean ...

  —What?

  —Never mind. It only happened once. I've gotten over it.

  — What only happened once?

  — I said never mind! So, what about your guy?

  —Eric? I don't know. He's not at all like the boys I dated in high school, that's for sure.

  —Is he an officer? You could bring him to the Club and we could have a double date. That'd be so bitchin'.

  —Yeah. Maybe not such a good idea right now.

I didn't fall asleep till way past midnight. What was bothering me was not at all my studies that I had been neglecting for over a week. I couldn't care less about them anymore. It wasn't the big question mark in my mind either ... should I move out of the Rush home and start living for myself? I had made up my mind to do that. I just needed to find a window to leave. What was keeping me up was having seen those men in the nightclub and knowing that some of them might be dead by spring. There was nothing that I could do about it though. There was nothing I could do about Eric either.

The window was opened thanks to Hiro, daddy, and through it I could take what Eric called my "great leap forward." Hiro's uncle, Nakano-san, who was the grandson of the founder of the Miyazawa Bookstore, mentioned to Hiro that he was looking for someone to sort and sell books for him for about five hours a day. Eric apparently told him that I might need a place to stay too and he said I could live in the room above the bookstore where there was a bathroom and a tiny kitchen area with a two-burner gas stove. The trouble was the Rushes. They would never let me leave if I asked them to. They'd see it as a betrayal of trust to you, daddy. Jeanette and even Fran were all for it though.

—Just walk out one day and don't come back.

—I couldn't do that. My father would have a cow.

(You see, I never considered anything up till then without thinking of you, daddy.)

—When he finds out about it, it will be a fait accompli.

—Where did you learn words like that, Fran? My little sister, and she's got a vocabulary like Charles van Doren.

—I read books, Jeanette, not just trashy magazines like you.

Jeanette just laughed right in her sister's face and I couldn't help but stifle a laugh too. Fran smiled and we all held hands and got the sniffles because we knew there and then that I was going to leave the house for good.

That night I wrote a letter to the Rushes thanking them for everything they'd done for me and giving them the telephone number of the bookstore. I wrote a letter to you, too, daddy, remember? About five days later you phoned me at the bookstore and ordered me to move back to the base and finish my studies, but I said that I just wanted to drop out of all that for a year and I promised you it would only be a year. What's a year out of my life now? I needed the freedom to find myself. You said something that hurt me very much then, daddy, something that cut right to the bone. You said, "Now I have two dropouts for children" and "If your mother were alive, Jeff and you, but especially you, wouldn't have done this to me." But I said I wasn't doing it to you, daddy. This had nothing to do with your life, nothing in the world. I pleaded with you, "It's about me and maybe for the first time in my life I am doing something that is just about me." You hung up on me. You just hung up on me, and I must tell you now, with you lying in front of me, eyes and lips shut like little trap doors, limbs like dead logs, that your hanging up on me was just awful. It was awful, daddy ... and I can still hear that deafening bang that came from you directly to me through the receiver. I wish I could wake you up right now with just such a bang, only a hundred times louder. I would send it into your brain like you sent it into mine until you sat up with your eyes open like saucers and your jaw dropped like an animal trap and you screamed at the top of your lungs. "Stop it! Stop it! STOP IT!" That's what I want to hear coming from your stiff lips, daddy, that's how I want you to feel for once in your life for slamming your receiver down on me like that. But I guess all I can wish for now is for you to hear me tell you this in your very appropriate silence. Are you going to give me a sign that you are hearing me whether you like it or not? You're doing everything in your power to shut me out again, aren't you.

What, is that a sigh I detect coming from you or just the faintest of breaths? And another one ... and another? Is this the sign then that you are taking in what I am telling you, that you really care about me, what has happened to me since the day I left "home" in September 1967, that you recognize my life as something more than an extension of your own, as something that exists in its own right? Do I disappoint you, daddy? Do I not live up to your name? Am I not going to be the woman my mother was? No, it couldn't be a sigh, not even a sigh of disappointment. You don't sigh, do you, daddy. Doctor George Rogers, president of the California Thoracic Association, one of the state's leading specialists on chests. Now you're the one who's not breathing at all, aren't you, daddy. Wait. No, even the merest undulation of your chest has stopped. Total stillness. Closest thing to death. Five, six, seven, eight seconds ... not a single breath ... how long can you keep this up? Ah, you got me there ... now deeply inhaling, a long slow intake of air through blue lips, like a tide of water pulling into shore, then exhaling in little spurts of air. Wait a sec. Again stillness, a *hiatus linguae*, you love words like that, don't you, daddy. See, we still have togetherness, we have togetherness in all things dead. Your static mouth, your cut tongue, your interrupted breath … six, seven, eight, nine seconds … inhaling again, even more deeply than a moment ago, that flow like the lightest foam … hold it in, daddy, you can do it, I know you can. Hold it … hold it … good going, way to go, daddy, now seal those blue lips, now gradually part them, that's it, you're doing a good job, daddy, you're holding your own with the best of them, your true-blue buddies at the L.A. Athletic Club would be proud of you, hey, Johnny Weissmuller would be proud of you, daddy, after all, didn't you rub shoulders with him in the pool and ask him to introduce you to Esther Williams? You'd've had a chance with her, daddy, what with your natural charm and your ways … your ways, daddy, oh those ways … we both know about those ways, don't we? … now a rush of air hisses out, attaboy, hole in one, daddy! Nothing else moves, though, daddy, not a bit of the old body. That body stood you in good stead, didn't it? Always was able to stand up and be counted on, right? Oh, wouldn't you like to now. Wouldn't you like to turn back the clock, say, well, to October 1967? I was gone a month by then, Jeff was rapidly turning himself into a shell in front of a pocked wall in Nepal, and you had a visitor, didn't you, daddy? Someone I sent to stay at our home on her way to New York. Mieko, ring a bell? Daughter of one of the base drivers. Mieko, Mieko, Mieko. Get a rise out of you? So, what would you do now if you could, eh? I know, you'd sit up, skoot yourself over to the edge of the bed and point a bent finger at me? Maybe you'd even call me to you so you could give me one of your famous hugs. You like to hug young girls, don't you? Oh, daddy, you must be seething inside yourself, locked up inside yourself, your mind a dungeon full of powerless white-sheeted ghosts, and all you can do is plaster yourself against the dull black wall of your nightmare hoping none of them will turn on you. I'm not going to let them lie, daddy! You hear?

—Good evening. Or should I say good morning. You must be the daughter.

I stood up and turned fully toward him. It was Dr. Price, the short, stocky intern in green.

—It's amazingly kind of you to sit up with him all night. Daughters these days just want to breeze in, kiss the old geezer on the forehead and make tracks. Has his catheter been looked at?

—Yes, Nurse Arden did it a couple of hours ago, I think.

Dr. Price walked to the foot of the bed.

—Let's have a look at his chart.

He has unhooked the clipboard with your medical chart on it, daddy, walking around the bed while rubbing his index finger under his nose, and now he's placed the clipboard on your chest where it's rocking gently. He's wiggling your nasogastric tube and stroking your forehead.

—Has he been breathing normally, that is, regularly?

I took a step back from the bed and rested my hands on the back of my chair.

—Yes. I think so. I've been watching him the whole time. He's the same as he was before.

Dr. Price smiled and stared at me for a moment.

—May I ask your name?

—Karen.

—Karen, hi, I'm Chuck, Chuck Price. It's originally not Price. It was Przybyszewski. Can't blame my father. No one in this country could say his name. Look, I'm here for you all night, you know. If there's anything at all you need, please just press the button and buzz me. Or course, if your father gets into difficulty, be sure to call me immediately.

He walked back around the bed, replacing the chart on its hook, and came right up to me, resting his hand on my arm.

—Just buzz me. I'll come right away.

I nodded and let go of the back of the chair. His palm slipped down my forearm, he squeezed my fingers and left.

You're breathing regularly again. I'm feeling tired down to my bones, daddy. Should I go on with this? Shouldn't I just drive back to Pacific Palisades and sleep in my old bed? Old bed? It's only been empty for nine months, everything is still there in my room where I left it, nothing has been so much as touched … my old stuffed toys, my record collection, my photo albums, my high school class sweater. I could slip back into that life, forget everything that happened to me in Japan, be the same person I always was. You'd like that, wouldn't you? That's what you want for me, isn't it, daddy? And you'll forgive me too, won't you? You'll say your little girl went astray like all little girls do, an encounter with the wrong kind of people, being led down a garden path by "bad elements," a wander in a dark forest, an adventure, sure, everybody wants to have at least one adventure in his life, a run-in with worthless and dangerous weirdos … someone borrows a few dollars from you and refuses to give them back, a man shoves you up against a wall and tells you never to do that again and you don't know what they're talking about, someone rushes up to you, the bogeyman streaking out from behind a tree, intent on carrying you away over his shoulder, taking you to a shack, kicking open the door, throwing you on the putrid bed and having his way with you, doing whatever he wanted and however he wanted it before devouring you … is that what you think happened to me? Okay, fine by me. It's no skin off my back, daddy. I'm not going to even try and control your spin on my life, your twisted angle, your "take," the perversions you imagine in the dark. You ought to know about perversions daddy, you ought to know about them better than anyone! Mieko was one, but not the first. Remember? Sure ya do! Your little Oktoberfest in the master bedroom? Are you recalling that now in your dark dungeon, going over the details, relishing the pictures of her flesh you've stored in your darkroom mind? I want you to recall everything you can, daddy. Don't leave out a thing, now. Don't let a single detail slip away. That's all I ask of you right now. Keep it all inside you and gloat. Gloat! Keep your back to the wall and watch the parade, daddy, your own sweet-smelling rose parade, your forced hole in one, your own little private celebration of brute force. Pity I'm the only one you can share it with. That's the pity. What good is a conquest if no one ever hears about it? My lips are sealed though. I won't tell a soul, ever. You saw and you conquered, daddy. Good going, buddy. And I saw and conquered too, daddy, and now I'm back to tell the tale to you because you really need to hear it, you really need to.

So I'm not going to let sleep get the better of me. I've got to finish what I'm going to say to you first. You may be a silent witness but you are a witness nonetheless, and you are going to soldier on until I decide it's over.

I took the great leap forward and moved into the little room above the bookstore in Jinbocho. I felt exhilarated. I'd be able to live on the money I took with me together with what I'd make by working. Your little practical girl had that part all planned out. Dr. Ben phoned and asked me what I was intending to do about my studies. I told him I would write a letter to the dean and tell him that I was discontinuing them, but Dr. Ben said that I would lose my student status and the right to remain in the country, and because the dean was a patient of his he would tell him I was temporarily withdrawing but planned to return to the campus in early '68. That way the police wouldn't come after me for being an illegal alien. I thanked him for that and he said that he was doing it for you, daddy, not for me. So you bear some responsibility for what happened to me after that. But I'm outside your dungeon now, daddy, and I've got the key right here in my hands. I can set you free now, daddy, no one else can, not even the doctors here. Free at last, daddy, free at last.

Nakano-san, the grandson of the founder of the Miyazawa Bookstore who speaks English with an English accent, took me around the stacks and told me to memorize where everything was. Back in the early 1900s they sold woodblock prints and Japanese art but by the 1920s or so they had gone over entirely to English-language books. Nakano-san explained that the reason his name was Nakano and not Miyazawa is that he was adopted into his wife's family and took on her name. How does that strike you, daddy? Maybe I'll marry a Japanese and he'll take on my name, like, Hiroshi Rogers or Noritake Rogers. Or maybe I'll marry a Negro, how about that? You think mom would turn over in her grave if I went and did it? Maybe you'll turn over on your bed right here in front of me. Hey, I'm going to marry a Negro! His spade skin will be all over me, daddy, his big thick lips will cover my mouth and he'll be deep into me, you'd like that, wouldn't you, your precious daughter "violated"? A violation requires a fine, see, a punishment. What would you do, daddy? Would you lash him with your forked tongue, would you deafen him with white profanities ... or would you want to hurt him, maim him? I'd like to know. It means a lot to me to hear what you would do to him. I'll tell you more, sure. You can't make a decision on the basis of a few bedside allegations, can you. How many like me were there in the village? They were wearing black pyjamas. Did our men disappear down dirt holes, following them? Did they run out of huts naked, girls too, when your boys set them on fire? They were sitting ducks, sure. They were begging to be taken, bound and blindfolded, weren't they. They asked for us to holler into their ears, to have our spit dripping down their necks, they asked for it, didn't they? So look the other way, daddy, make known your might, the deeds your men have done, for the same thing's happened to your little girl, hasn't it? I've been taken too by some wicked force. Sure, I know what you'd be thinking ... she'll get over it ... she'll put it all down to experience, a fleeting nightmare brushed away by the light. I'm your sunshine, your little sunshine, I make you happy when skies are black. But no black is going to extinguish my light, is it, daddy? That's the way you see it, isn't it, a temporary eclipse? You would never admit to yourself that it wasn't a violation at all, that I came to him of my own free will, that I gave myself to him because I wanted to. I craved him. That's the way it was, daddy. I craved him more than I have craved anything in my life.

Eric came into the store on my first Saturday of work to buy a book. It was a book on the history of Negroes in entertainment by Langston Hughes. I'd never heard of him. Eric had seen the book in the store a few weeks earlier and had decided to buy it. Put one more S in the U.S.A. Then the U.S.A. would be like the U.S.S.R. That's from a poem, daddy. Not to your taste really. I don't think we should open up a discussion here at your sickbed on contemporary Negro poetry. I'm not into one-way conversations. I'm getting all sorts of good vibrations from you here and I'm not about to spoil it by getting bogged down in poetics. We better stick to things close to home, don't you think, things that happened to you and me because we're connected, everything that happens to you happens to me and everything that happened to me happens to you, isn't that right? There's a silk thread that connected us across the Pacific and I ravelled it up by coming back, got it all tangled and clustered with knots.

I'm undoing that ball of thread right now. It's sitting here on the bed between us. When I get it all untangled I'm going to weave it up just for you into the smoothest fabric and place that fabric over your face so that you can feel it against your skin and breathe in its odors. That fabric is the story of both our lives, daddy, a silk shroud laid straight on top of your face. You may not be able to see it through your trapdoor lids but you'll smell it, won't you? Breathe in that fragrance in one of those long breaths of yours. Take it inside yourself because one fine morning you're not going to be able to let it out. It's going to stay deep inside you. The pungent odor of the fabric of all those many connected threads may remain with you till kingdom come.

Hiro rushed into the store. He was wearing a dented helmet with Japanese characters written in black on it and was carrying a long thick stick in gloved hands. He had a stream of caked blood running from the back of his ear down his neck. His uncle was out to lunch and I was alone in the store. I took him to my room upstairs, removed his shirt and washed the blood that had flowed down to the middle of his back. When he had sufficiently calmed down he told me that the Kidotai had closed in on a small demonstration he was marching in not far away at Kudanshita. I didn't know what the Kidotai was and he told me it was the riot police. He asked where Eric was and I said he was here earlier but went out on some errand, I didn't know where. Just then I heard the little bell above the door that rings when someone comes into the store and I said to Hiro I would be back in a minute and went downstairs. It was Eric followed a few steps behind by Hiro's uncle, Nakano-san. I beckoned with my finger for Eric to come upstairs and asked Nakano-san if I could take my lunch break and he said yes.

When Eric and I got to the room Hiro was sitting in a lotus

position on the tatami facing the window. Eric sat beside him, putting his arm around him, and Hiro laid his head on Eric's shoulder. I made green tea for the three of us and we sat facing each other on the tatami in the middle of the room. They could see that I didn't have a clue as to what was going on.

—It's about Anpo. The Zengakuren, that's the student movement, is getting more active because the Japanese government is repressing any opposition.

—What's Anpo, Eric?

—Jesus, Karen.

—I did study American history, you know, Eric. I did a term paper in my freshman year on the Marshall Plan.

–Well, this is a little different from the Marshall Plan. Anpo is the security treaty between Japan and the U.S. Without that America couldn't keep up the war in Vietnam. America needs the money and support of the Japanese, the bases, the R&R.

—No, Eric, the R&R guys go to Korea and Taiwan where the girls are cheaper. Your Uncle Sam likes to save money when he can. Emi has interviewed some of the girls there.

—Where is Emi, Hiro?

—I was separated from her at the demo. She's one of our leaders. We're meeting up later in Shinjuku. Want to join us?

—Yeah, sure. I've got to be back at Zama by 10:00, though.

—What about you, Karen?

—Yeah, I guess so. If Eric's going.

Hiro gulped his tea down and put his shirt back on.

—Can I leave my *gevabo* and helmet here?

—The *gevabo* is his stick.

—Yeah, I get that much, Eric. Sure, why not?

—Thanks a lot, Karen. Thanks, Eric. See you both tonight. You know where to go, don't you Eric? Mecca. Same place as before.

—Yeah, the coffee shop. We'll be there at about 6:30 or

thereabouts.

—Great. See you.

After Hiro left I could see that Eric was restless. He stood in the corner by the window looking down on the street and shaking his head.

—What's the matter, Eric?

—I don't know. Things are going to come to a head. I kind of feel it in my bones.

—What things? What do you mean?

—Things at the base and in Japan. Some of our guys are being shipped out already.

—To Vietnam?

—Yeah. They're scared shitless, at least the ones I know, but there's nothing they can do.

—Maybe the war will be over soon. They'll be all right.

—Fat chance of that, Karen. Over soon, that's a good one. How many Viet Cong are they going to kill before we call it quits?

We sat down on the tatami. He stretched his legs out and laid his head in my lap. I felt so much that I wanted to put my hand on his head and stroke his hair, daddy, but I didn't.

—You'll have to go too, won't you?

—Do you want me to?

He half sat up, turned his head toward me, looked into my eyes and repeated his question.

—No.

He sat up and crossed his legs. His knees were touching mine. He took both my hands in his and brought them to his lips. I could see tears welling in his eyes.

—What is it, Eric?

—I don't know. I didn't expect this to happen.

—What to happen?

—Meeting you. Maybe having met you is making it harder

for me to accept the fact that I … I mean, uh, before now, I think I could have gotten myself to …

Tears were now streaming down his cheeks. He clamped his lips shut and held my fingers against them. Two or three tears dropped onto the back of my hands. I should have taken him in my arms, daddy. God knows I wanted to. But something was holding me back, maybe something about me being white and him being black.

—This is ridiculous. Soldiers aren't supposed to blubber like this, especially before they even know if they're going to be sent to war.

—You're brave, that's why you're crying.

—Brave? Is stealing away from the base at every chance I get brave? Is preferring to spend time with Japanese who hate what we Americans are doing brave? And what if I'm given the order to go to Vietnam? It's bound to happen. Is it brave to bite the bullet and go and kill innocent people, people who have no grievance with us and who just want to be left alone in their own country? What's brave, that's what I'd like to know.

It was the first time for me that anything to do with politics had a connection with a real person I knew … or with me. Before then it had just been discussions and arguments about different ideas, what Prof. Cromwell called "scenarios." I put my arms around Eric, daddy, and drew him close to me, right up against my breasts. I wanted to protect him. He kissed me, and the most exquisite sensation of warmth poured all over my skin. He was the one who broke the kiss. I didn't want it to end.

—What's the matter, Eric? I'm sorry.

—No, I'm sorry. Man, I am so so sorry.

—Why?

—Because you have no idea what you're getting yourself into. No idea. This whole thing is way above my head, above all our heads. It's like a flood that's coming. I don't want you to drown in it too. I don't want to pull you under.

—Look, I'm not a child. My decisions, if I take them, are my own.

—Are they? What about your father?

—He's not here, is he?

That's what I said, daddy. That's what came out. I want you to know that. I knew how furious you would be with me, kissing a Negro and not only a Negro but a soldier "bent on cowardice, like those hippies who throw flowers in cops' faces and think it's funny." Oh, I remember your every word. Each and every one of those words was branded by you on the surface of my brain. "The world is an evil place, Karen … the world is full of traps … and there are people in the world, many people, who envy and hate us, don't you forget that, Karen, they despise us for what we have achieved … your mother and I always wanted what was best for you … your mother and I wanted to shield you so that you could go through life without having to meet up with evil, with traps set by people who will exude goodwill but harbor evil toward you. They are out there, Karen, everywhere you will go when you leave this country. Envy and hatred will appear to you in benign guises, but behind those guises is venom, Karen, venom that, once inside you, can poison your free will. Up till now we have shielded you from that venom. We don't want it to get inside you."

Venom, daddy? How does it get inside me? In the saliva from a Negro's mouth? Is it rubbed by black hands into my soft white flesh like lotion? Or is it words, daddy, words that refute what you say and call it a pack of lies, words that cause the red and black brands you burnt into the surface of my brain to turn gray and fade away? Is it sights of another place, a place that, in time, starts to look normal, though it is so completely different from anything a girl has seen before? Or is the vapor of a venom carried through the air that you breathe with other people who are not at all like you, and suddenly your life is affected and you cannot distinguish your fate from theirs ... their life from day to day has become inextricably interwoven with yours, and though they are total strangers, their blood comes to mean more to you than that of your "own people." That venom is blood, daddy. That's what it is. It's blood! Mixed blood!

Did that disturb you? Is breathing the primary means of communication you have with me? If so, then you *do* hear me. You're even coughing and wheezing and now you're clamping up your lips tight again ... nine, ten, eleven, twelve whole seconds, daddy, between breaths. That's one hell of a long hiatus. I hear you, daddy, I hear you in those intermittent breaths. You're saying, "You are killing me, Karen. You are striking at my heart with your little stories. You are taking advantage of me. You are suffocating me with these vile words of yours."

But it's not stories, daddy. It really happened to me all the time I was away. And as God is my witness, I am not trying to suffocate you. On the contrary, I want to breathe new life into you. I want you to take in what I say as if my words were oxygen. I want you to come to life, daddy. I want you to place your hand on mine and say, "You have opened my eyes, sweetheart, and now I can see. I see what a wonderful and beautiful and spectacular woman you have turned into and I recognize that I had nothing to do with it. You did it yourself. You have come into your own and a father could ask for nothing more."

But you can't open your eyes, you can't put your hand on mine. You just lie there as if you were taking your last breaths, and I know what you're thinking. You're thinking about that venom that has wormed its way into me. Oh yes, Eric fucked me, daddy. He certainly did. That's what you really wanted to know, isn't it? But not that day and not for some time and not until I wanted him to so much I would have given up everything precious to me to have him inside me. I needed that venom that he shot into me, daddy. It didn't stop there. It coursed through my entire body, through my veins, until it got into the deepest parts of my skull. And when it did, the brands that you left on my brain washed away and vanished forever. I'd cut open my skull for you, daddy, right here and now at your bedside if I thought you'd see for yourself. But you can't see, can you. You're not going to open your eyes, are you. You're not going to give me a sign. You're just going to stop breathing when the time comes. That's the only freedom you've got left. Good for you, daddy. Okay, you've made your point, I can see that.

You're breathing more calmly now. You've made your little threats in the air. You're a doctor, after all, and doctors can get their point through loud and clear without even saying a word. "If you continue like this I'll die on you." I know what's in your mind. I've peeked into that dungeon often enough. Ah, but even so you're not at peace with yourself, are you. My "little stories" pain you. That's the rub, isn't it … my freedom, your pain? Well, daddy, you ain't heard nothin' yet. Isn't that what the man said? We've got all night, you and me. So save your breath!

Eric not only calmed down, he seemed elated. He started to tell me about his family, mainly his brother. I wanted to tell him about Jeff, but I had to get back to work downstairs. Eric asked if he could stay just until the evening.

—Sure. Pull out my futon and get some shuteye.

—You're an angel.

—Yeah, that's what my dad says. I don't think either of you knows me.

—Thank you so much, Karen. I'll just cuddle up to Hiro's big stick. Oh, that didn't sound so good.

That afternoon Nakano-san asked me to restack the Japanese

art book section. I asked about two large art books in plastic covers on the glassed-in shelves behind the counter.

—Do these go in the bookcases.

—No. These are books of Shunga. They are not for everyone.

—Shunga?

—Yes. It means "spring pictures." But they are, how do you say, racy?

—Racy? You mean they're about, uh, physical things?

—Yes. I do not think it appropriate for a young woman to see them.

Quite a few customers came into the store, about half of them foreigners, and it wasn't until after four that I finished the restacking.

—I am going out for approximately a quarter of an hour, Karen-san. If a customer comes in and you cannot help them, please tell them to await my return.

I couldn't see the front door from where I was standing, but I heard the bell ring and the door shut. I immediately went to the shelves behind the counter, slid open the glass, pulled down one of the Shunga books and opened it. The page on the left showed a man with an enormous penis and very hairy testicles having intercourse with a woman whose intricately decorated kimono was open in a V shape to expose her huge gaping vagina. Another woman in kimono, whose index and middle finger were inside her own vagina, was looking on. The toes of the woman having intercourse were curled in. On the right-hand page was a picture of a naked woman on her back being ravished by a giant octopus. The tip of one of its tentacles was wrapped around the nipple of her left breast and the enormous lips of its mouth were flush against her hairy vagina. The woman's eyes were shut tight and her head was thrown back in ecstasy. But the amazing thing about the picture was the head of the octopus. It was bald, like a monk's, and the octopus' black-and-white eyes were wide open, as if it was seeing a world it had never ever imagined before. The picture's title was "The Dream of the Fisherman's Wife." The front bell rang and a young Western man wearing thick glasses entered. I hurriedly replaced the book on the shelf and slid the glass shut.

—Can I help you?

—Yes. I am looking for a book on temple bells. Do you have one, by chance?

He had an accent that sounded German.

—Oh, I'm not sure. I'm sorry, I haven't been working here that long. Do you mind browsing in the art book section? Or maybe it would be in architecture. I'll have a look there. The owner will be back in a jiffy.

—A jiffy?

—Yes, soon.

—Are you living here long?

—No.

—I am here for three and a half years. Are you American?

—Yes.

—I have been in your country, at Ann Arbor in the state of Michigan.

—I've never been there. In fact, I've never been east of the Grand Canyon.

—I see. I have never been there. But I have been to the Yarlung Zangbo in China. This is bigger and more deep going.

The bell over the front door rang and Nakano-san returned.

He put down a large hemp bag and approached us.

—This gentleman is looking for a book on temple bells.

—Temple bells? I regret to inform you that we have no such book here. We did have one, but it sold more than a year ago. I am truly sorry.

—This is okay. Thank you.

I went to the front door, which hadn't shut properly, and was about to push it closed when the man came up behind me. I opened the door for him.

—Thank you so much. Do you work here every day? I could come again.

—Uh, well, not really. I'm just helping out.

—I see. Okay, I see. Thank you so much.

When I returned to the counter I saw Nakano-san touching the binding of the Shunga book I had replaced on the shelf behind the counter. He gently pushed it in, aligning it with the book next to it. He turned toward me. I detected a faint smile on his lips, but I couldn't be sure. I wasn't able then to read Japanese faces like I can now.

At five I went upstairs to my room. Nakano-san asked me to take the hemp bag and leave it on the landing halfway up the stairs. It was very heavy. When I entered my room Eric was fast asleep with Hiro's helmet on his chest. The big stick was leaning against the wall in the corner. I picked up my purse, inadvertently rattling my keys in it. Eric bolted up, breathing heavily.

—Oh, I got a fright.

—Sorry. I was trying to be as quiet as I could.

—Oh my God, it's already, like, five. I shouldn't have slept so long.

—You needed it, Eric. You were exhausted. You're under such a strain, I don't know how you put up with it.

—I put up with it because I can share it with you.

He smiled a big smile at me, showing all his teeth.

—See? Look. They do look whiter, don't they?

—What do you mean?

—Oh, never mind, it's just a bad joke. Listen, let's go now. We can catch a bite before we meet Hiro. I know a groovy noodle place near Shinjuku Station.

—Okay, let me just make myself presentable.

He laughed.

—Baby, you look plenty presentable, oh yeah.

—Thanks, but it's a way of my saying that I want to use the bathroom.

—Okay, I get it. I'll just wait outside.

—Thanks. I'll be ready before you can say Jackie Robinson. Uh-oh, did I say the wrong thing?

—You can't say the wrong thing, not to me, Karen. I'll just be outside.

After I went to the bathroom and freshened myself up, I called to Eric.

—You can come in now. I'm decent.

Eric shut the door. He took me in his arms and kissed me passionately, putting his tongue into my mouth.

—Oh, you'll muss me all up. Uh, have you seen my muffler? Oh, there it is, behind the chair. It's from Phelps Wilger.

—Don't get it. Who's that guy? Phelps somebody?

—Phelps Wilger? It's an exclusive men's shop in L.A. It's 100% cashmere. Feel it.

—Ooo, dat's smooth, man.

—Come on, don't make fun of me. I didn't buy it. It was a going away present for me from my father.

—Yeah, he wanted you to keep it around your neck.

—Eric, there you go again. He's not an ogre, you know.

—Whoever said he was? Not every Republican is bad, I recognize that. Is he a John Bircher?

—I don't know, but he's an Elk.

—Okay. Hey, what's that bag doing out there on the landing?

—That's Nakano-san's. He asked me to bring it up.

—Did you have a look inside?

—Of course not.

—There are handouts in it, lots of them.

—Handouts?

—Yeah, printed flyers.

—What do they say?

—I don't know. I can't read Japanese. But it sure looks like they're something to do with America and Anpo, like, smash it up or something like that. Now, how do you want to get to Shinjuku?

—We can't keep taking cabs, Eric, if that's what you mean. Look, let's walk to Suidobashi Station, it's only ten minutes away, then take the Kokutetsu to Shinjuku on the Chuo-Sobu Line.

—Holy smoke, you said that as if you've lived here for years. Impressive stuff, baby, impressive. Kokutetsu, the national railways. Even with the right accent.

—A girl learns fast.

—I think you're right at home here already.

—Part of me is.

When we left my room a few minutes later the bag was gone from the landing. Walking to the station I asked Eric about his family again.

—It must have been awful for your parents to lose a son. And for you.

—It devastated us all. Did I tell you about Scotland?

—No, you mentioned Europe, though.

—Yeah, same trip. We hiked all over Scotland. You know Glencoe?

—No, should I?

—I was fourteen and Gordon was about sixteen. We climbed up this sheer rock mountain like it was some monumental overturned cauldron. It was so quiet there, a really apt silence, know what I mean? Sound would have intruded into that landscape. We stood shoulder to shoulder, kind of clinging to each other, I guess, and the sky was all gray like cinder, like ash, like the inside of a furnace that had burned out ages and ages ago and, I swear, the wind was whipping us like icicles or something and, you know, if we had let go of each other even for a second we would have been swept right down the face of that cliff, the two of us, right then and there. I can still feel the warmth of his body against mine and … oh, shit, there I go getting all blubbery again. Karen, I think you got one big black crybaby on your hands.

—Maybe I like crybabies. You lost your brother, Eric. You have a right to cry.

—Yeah. It's one of the few rights I've still got, I guess.

—I mean, those white thugs killed him, didn't they? Of course you're upset. People never get over these sorts of things.

—Look, I don't want to talk about it. You keep asking me about my family. I mean, you got a brother too, don't you?

—Yes. Jeff. He's in Nepal.

—So, what the hell's he doing there?

—Meditating. He's got a beard too. Looks like …

—Abe Lincoln's?

—Yeah, only kind of … wispier. If my dad saw the snap of him that I have with that beard he'd blow a gasket.

—Pretty volatile, your dad?

—Only when it comes to me and my brother. Otherwise he's always composed.

—Composed, I like that. Wish I was more composed. So, Nepal. I hope he isn't workin' his mojo out there.

—His what?

—Mojo. Drugs. A lot of the guys at Zama get their stuff from people in Nepal or people who've been through there. It's a breeze.

—I don't think Jeff would be doing that.

—I sure hope not. It's a bad scene, Karen. I've seen it.

After having ramen in Shinjuku 3-chome we went to a coffee

shop called Mecca around the corner from an art movie house to meet up with Hiro. Emi was there, and when we walked in she glanced up at me squinting her eyes as if to say to Eric, "Why did you bring her here?" She obviously didn't trust me, probably thinking that I would betray her to someone at an American base.

—Hey, Hiro, how's it going?

—Hi, Eric. Hello, Karen.

Emi closed a compact notebook and put it in her purse.

—Emi. Good to see you.

—Thank you, Eric. Good to see you, too.

There was not a single unoccupied seat in Mecca, and almost everybody was smoking, including Hiro and Emi. Hiro stubbed out his cigarette.

—So, what's happening, Eric?

—Everyone says there's going to be another huge build-up, putting our troops at over half a million. And one of our guys who came back from Saigon to Zama just two days ago said some troops went into a small hamlet and went sort of berserk on the women and children.

The waiter came up to our table and Hiro ordered for us.

—*Kohi futatsu.* (Two coffees.)

The waiter picked up some empty plates at the next table and walked back to the counter. Emi put out her cigarette and lit another one with a silver lighter.

—It's not the first time.

—First time for what?

—That your soldiers have gone berserk in a Vietnamese village. Berserk. Hmm. Nice euphemism for a massacre.

—Man, Emi, I can't get over your English. It's better than mine.

—Emi went to high school in L.A., that's why.

—No need to talk about that, Hiro.

—L.A.? Really? Gosh, that's where I'm from.

Emi looked at me blankly.

—Where were you in L.A., Emi? That's amazing.

—It was years ago. I'm much older than you two.

She pointed to Eric and Hiro. She didn't even include me in the calculation.

—Oh gosh, but that's so neat. Which high school? I was at Palisades High.

—Manual Arts. You wouldn't know it, would you.

—Manual Arts? But all the kids there are poor Negroes.

No sooner had I said that than I realized how stupid a comment it was.

—Sorry, Eric. That didn't come out like I meant it.

—That's fine. If it's true, what's the big deal?

Emi put out her cigarette and tossed the lighter into the purse hanging on the back of her chair.

—Negro, Mexican and Japanese. Black, brown and yellow, with a few grains of salt mixed in just for good measure.

The waiter came carrying two coffees on a wooden tray, his body cleaving the smoke as he moved toward us.

—Emi's off to Hanoi day after tomorrow.

Eric looked really taken aback by hearing this.

—Hanoi?

—Yes, Eric. Why? Does that shock you? I've been there once before. The spirit there is wonderful. They know they're going to win, no matter how many Americans come to invade. Half a million, a million … it doesn't matter. It just means that more Americans are going to go home in body bags or without an arm, a leg or an eye.

—Well, we don't want that, man, but we do want the war to end as soon as possible.

—You may not want it, Eric, but that's the upshot. I've talked to young Vietnamese men, some of them just boys, who'd been blinded by chemicals dropped on them in American bombs. I've talked with women who'd lost husbands and fathers and brothers in the fighting and were still full of hope. What for, that's what I wanted to know. What is it all for? There was a wrecked American helicopter on display and ...

Eric took a sip of coffee, looking away. Hiro broke in.

—Yeah, well, whatever happens, the fewer people who get killed the better, on all sides.

It was almost as if Hiro wanted to change the subject, perhaps out of deference to Eric and me. For a moment no one said anything. Eric just sipped his coffee.

—I could be in one of those helicopters one of these days.

I felt Eric's hand rest on my knee under the table and grabbed it, squeezing it hard. If we had been alone I know that I would have started to cry.

Hiro put his hand on Eric's shoulder.

—Just don't go, Eric. Just come to us and we'll get you out some way or other. We've got friends who are talking about getting some American soldiers to Sweden through the Soviet Union.

—Naw, I don't want to do that. That's not my bag.

—Why not?

—Don't know. Just don't want to. I'd never be able to go back to the States.

Emi stood, throwing her purse over her shoulder.

—I've got to go. There's a meeting at Golden-gai.

She put eighty yen on the table.

—This is for my coffee. See you.

A cold wind rushed through the room when she opened the door, sending folds of smoke to each side like a curtain opening.

—Emi's the leader of a cell. Without her we'd just be a bunch of quibbling little boys aching for a fight. She gives us focus.

—She's amazing, Hiro. But I feel she really hates me.

—Hates you? Why should she hate *you*, Karen?

—I don't know. Maybe she sees me as the enemy.

Hiro took a 100-yen note out of his pocket and put it on the table.

—More like class enemy. She doesn't have anything against Americans.

—Class? I'm not sure what you mean by that, Hiro.

—You tell her, Eric. I've got to get home and make supper for my grandma.

Hiro left. Eric shook his head, smiling at me.

—Money, baby, just money. That's what it's all about. That's what it's for, this whole goddamn war. We're soldiers of fortune, whether we like it or not. Or, soldiers of misfortune would be more like it. How much is one life worth, huh?

I suddenly felt as if I couldn't breathe in that room and started to cough. Eric stood.

—Let's split. Worst thing about this country. They're going to kill more people with cigarette smoke than all the bombs you can drop on anybody.

We took a detour through Golden-gai on our way back to Shinjuku Station. The narrow alleys were lined with tiny bars and cafes, some of them looking no bigger than a telephone booth. Because of the crowds pushing both ways, we were carried straight ahead as if in a line we couldn't get out of.

—Hey look, there's Emi.

Eric pointed into one of the bars that had its door ajar. The counter sat about six people and there were only three small round tables between it and the door. Emi was standing at one of the tables gesturing and making some sort of speech to the young people packed into the bar. She didn't seem to notice us as we were gradually swept along by the line of people behind us. We came to an open area where there was a shrine. Beside the shrine a huge red tent was pitched with a long line of people waiting to get in.

—Look, Eric, must be for some sort of show.

Eric didn't even look. Instead he put his arms around me and started to kiss me. I pulled my head back.

—Hey, what's the matter?

—Nothing. It's just that it's not the custom here. People don't kiss in public here. Not even husbands and wives.

—Yeah okay, but we're not Japanese, so.

—No. But we're living here. This is their country.

He stepped back as if to observe me.

—My goodness me.

That's all he said, daddy, "My goodness me." Was he pleasantly surprised that I had come to realize where I was, that Tokyo was not L.A. and not San Diego or any other city in the United States? Or was he shocked that I was about to lose a grip on myself, to relegate everything that went into making me the person I am to some old rusted chest with a stubborn lock in an attic, not to be rediscovered and opened for decades, and when it is, it is marvelled over in disbelief ... could this have been me? Did I ever really look like this, act like this, talk like this, believe like this? I'm leaving the chest with you, daddy, with the rotten key that still opens it. Open it whenever your heart desires. Take out the dresses, especially the blueberry dress, smell the odors that come out of the chest and revel in them, revel in the words you will hear resonating in your head when you look deep into the old chest ... those are the words you heard coming out of my mouth long long ago, those words, daddy, that you and everybody put into my mouth, those odors that you sprayed over my body like nickel-and-dime perfume, those dresses that you and mom dressed me up in to get me ready for the ball, the grand ball that you imagined me dancing at for the rest of my life. If you want your little girl back, keep that old key to yourself, keep it forever and don't you let anybody tell you that your precious little American girl isn't still in there raring to come out and say, "Daddy, I'm home! Daddy, I'm back home. It's me, daddy, I'm home again!"

Now, don't go having one of those breathing spells on me, will you? Oh good, it was only a single hiatus, an isolated incident. We can cope with isolated incidents, can't we? We're breathing normally again now, aren't we? Everything's hunky-dory, a-okay. Here, daddy, let me adjust your pillow, maybe that will make it easier for you. How's that? Push your head back into the pillow as far as you can. Come on, daddy, you can do it. Push back. Harder. Pull that chin in. Pull in your chin, daddy! Good going. Everybody would be proud of you now to see you holding your head up high with your chin down as far as it can go. Now breathe, daddy, breathe. Come on, one … two … buckle your boot … that's the spirit. You're back on track now, daddy. You're with me here. And I know you're listening. Oh yes, you're all ears. The drip going into the crook of your elbow's doing its job, keeping you alive, if not exactly kicking. All our boys have drips, daddy, not just you. You're not special. It's one man, one drip. That's democracy in the U.S. of A., daddy, and don't you forget it.

When I returned to my room above the bookstore I found a little cloth bag hanging from the doorknob. In the bag there was a brown envelope with "Karen-san" written on it, and in the envelope four 1,000-yen bills, my wages for the week, and a note from Nakano-san thanking me for "a great start." I was exhausted and went to sleep without showering but not before taking Hiro's helmet off my futon and placing it in the corner beside his stick. I slept in my bra and undies, and the last thing

I remember is inhaling the odor of Eric's hair on my pillow.

The next day was a Sunday and I met Jeanette on the Ginza. I took her to a soba restaurant around the corner from the Hattori Clocktower Building.

—Wow, this is the first time I've had Japanese noodles.

—You don't get off the base much, do you.

—Almost never. Except sometimes when someone takes me, like to a coffee shop. But it's always in Tachikawa, near the base. Dad and mom don't like me to stray. They think I'll do something.

—Look, Jeanette. See those two Japanese women in the hats, long dresses and high heels?

—Yeah, bitchin'. I'd like to wear something like that, just once in my life.

—Oh, you will.

—You think so? I'd like for John to see me like that once. Then maybe he'd ...

—He'd what? Is that the guy you're going steady with?

—Not steady. We're just dating. He's nice most of the time.

—What do you mean most of the time?

—I don't want to talk about it. He takes me to this coffee shop where they serve liquor too. We drink beer there and a Japanese woman reads poetry in English with a jazz band playing. We haven't done anything, I swear.

—Okay. Right.

—We haven't! Just necking, no petting or anything like that. He's nice, he's really nice. He respects me. He took me to the movies. Have you seen "The Graduate"?

—No. Is it good?

—Really good. The guy rescues the girl just at the very end.

—How's Fran?

—The same only more obnoxious. She really needs some

guidance now but mom and dad are never around. Dad's really got his hands full with all the boys coming back from Vietnam in such bad shape, and mom's always off doing her clubs. The canasta club, the golf club, and they have this charity that looks after kids whose dads were Americans but just abandoned them kind of with their Japanese wives or mistresses and went back home. They're mostly half-Negro kids, I mean. They don't, you know, look after their families like we do.

—Yeah.

—Anyways, thanks ever so much for the noodles. They're great. So, when are you coming back for a visit? It seems like ages already.

—I'd like that. Christmas, maybe.

—Please do. Kimiko talks about you all the time.

—I really ought to see her.

—We all miss you, Karen.

—I miss you too, Jeannie.

I paid 120 yen for the two sobas and we walked, holding hands, back to the subway station.

—Look after yourself, Karen. I think what you're doing is tremendous. I wish I had the guts.

We hugged.

—You too, Jeannie. Bye.

I watched her descend into the station, then turned back toward the Clocktower Building. Despite all the cars spewing out their smoky fumes, the air was crisp and clear, not at all like the air in L.A. I breathed in deeply, daddy, real deeply. I felt that air kind of flushing me out inside. So, you can blame it on the air, too, if you want to. I strode down the Ginza, swinging my arms, and kept going like that until I had crisscrossed every single street, up and down, back and forth, noticing all the people, how they were dressed, how they moved their arms and legs, how they looked up at the buildings around them and how they stood perfectly still while waiting. I didn't stop walking until dark. Can you see me there in the dark? Can you distinguish me in the Japanese crowd? I bet you can't, daddy. I bet you couldn't find me among all those people, even though I don't look like them, don't talk like them, don't move my body like them and don't stand so perfectly still like them. I had disappeared into a crowd where I knew I could find myself.

By the middle of December I hadn't seen or spoken with Eric for over a week. I had found myself missing him in a way I had never missed anybody before. I had become accustomed to work at the bookstore, and Nakano-san was allowing me to use the cash register. He sometimes left the store for a few hours in the early afternoon, our least busy time. Sometimes he came back with his hemp bag full of flyers.

The 17th of December was a Saturday. A little after three, two young Western men, one very tall and gawky and the other stocky and so short he barely came up to his friend's neck, entered the shop. I could tell in a minute that they were Americans by their crewcuts, the neck of their T-shirts showing below their button-down collar check shirts, white cotton socks and pants that were much too short for them. I was alone in the store. The short one did the talking.

—Hey, hi there.

—Can I help you?

—Uh, yeah, I think so. We're looking for a book.

—What kind of book?

—Hey, you work here?

—Yes.

—Too much. What's your name?

—Exactly what kind of book were you looking for?

—Oh, I get it. Sure. Well, Chuck here and I are, uh, studying warfare. We'd like something on Japanese planes, you know, the Zero and stuff.

I led them to our military section.

—So, are you living here, like for real?

—Yes.

—Too much. We're out at Camp Zama. Know that?

I looked away from him, scanning the spines of some nearby books.

—Do you know Camp Zama?

—Yes.

—We don't get off the base much. But I really dig this city. Can you tell us where to go, I mean, when it gets dark? A guy needs a bit of R&R.

—I wouldn't know that sort of thing.

—Really? And you been living here? What do y'all do, you know, when it gets dark?

Luckily another customer, a Japanese, had just come through the front door. I was literally saved by the bell.

—Excuse me.

—Yeah, sure.

The other customer took one look at the books, said *Aa, sumimasen* (Oh, sorry) and walked out. I guess he had expected us to be a bookstore that carried Japanese books.

—So, you know, Chuck here and I were thinking that maybe, just maybe, you would show us around tonight, seeing as we're real greenhorns when it comes to Tokyo. We've got plenty of wampum.

He pulled a thick wad of American dollars from his pocket and fanned it in front of his face.

—Hey, Frank, those'd be no good here, buddy.

—Sure they are. Everybody loves American dollars wherever you go, isn't that right? Remember in Haiti, Chuck? A couple of bucks went a long way there, and I mean a real long way.

—Well, look, I wouldn't know, and actually I'm rather busy. If you can't find your book here, perhaps you can find it elsewhere in Jinbocho. There are plenty of …

—Where's that?

—Here. This is Jinbocho, for your information.

—Whoah now, you don't have to get all hostile on us, lady. No one was pushing you or anything.

—Let's split, Frank. Come on.

—Yeah. Bad news is bad news.

He stuffed the wad of bills back into his pocket and stared at me.

—If you change your mind, we'll be around. Toodeloo.

The two of them left. I leaned against the counter by the cash register and started sobbing. I stopped for a few seconds and peered out the store window at the people walking by. A Japanese girl in school uniform paused in front of the store and looked straight at me. She bowed her head once and, when I could see her face again, she was smiling. I smiled and bowed back to her, but by the time I had raised my head she was gone.

I gazed around the room. Shelves climbing up to the ceiling were stacked with old books, most of them from England and America. Where was Eric? Why hadn't he at least phoned me at the store? Had something happened to him? Maybe he was shipped out to Vietnam without warning, without having even a minute to phone me. If so, I would get a letter from him, one of those letters girls get from their boyfriends or husbands who've gone off to war, how they're in danger every day but nothing is going to happen to them, how they care about their buddies so much they'd give their life up for them, how much they miss "their girl." I didn't ever want to see one of those letters, daddy. I vowed that I would write to Eric and tell him, "Don't send me one of those letters, ever. Don't send me anything. I will just wait until you come back. I want you here with me. I don't want to hear from you from there."

The tears welled up in my eyes again and I felt an acid-like burning in the back of my throat. I spoke to myself. "Don't go, don't go. I don't want you to go. I don't want you to go!" It was then that the door opened and Nakano-san returned together with Hiro, both carrying large cardboard boxes. I turned away from them and wiped my cheeks with the back of my hand. Hiro came up behind me.

—Karen, Eric's coming later. He's really sorry he hasn't been in touch.

Hiro and Nakano-san went around the counter, put the boxes down and spoke softly with each other. I couldn't follow their conversation, although I could pick out a few words ... *Kyushu*, *ichigatsu*. They were talking about something in Kyushu happening in January.

—I've got to go now, Karen. But Eric's coming here at six and he told me to ask you to wait for him.

—Thank you, Hiro.

Just as Hiro left, the two American soldiers came through the door again.

—Thanks for holding the door, buddy. Hey, Chuck, she's still here. Uh-oh, looks like the manager's here too.

—May I help you, gentlemen?

—Uh yeah, maybe. Do you have a book on the battleship Yamato, you know the big one that sunk when ...

—Yes, I do know what the Yamato is. As a matter of fact, we have an excellent book about that tragic ship.

Nakano-san went to the military section to fetch the book.

—Hey, look, we were thinking, maybe we'd come back at around six and take you out for a bite, Japanese meal, anything. We'd like to try Japanese food and we know jackshit about it. So, how about it? Just a friendly dinner, nothing else. Cross my heart and hope to die.

—Thank you, but I am busy tonight. I won't be here at six.

—Well, five then.

—No. I said I'm not here.

—All right, you don't have to get all huffy under the collar about it. We're just hanging loose here, that's all. So, take it easy, babe.

They turned and walked toward the front door.

—Here is your book. This is the best book in English on the subject and it is in very excellent condition.

The short American went up to him.

—Keep it for the next war, friend.

The tall American guffawed, and they walked out without closing the door.

I finished work at five and went to a little grocery store in nearby Takebashi. Thousands of people were rushing about in the twilight, most of them on their way to one of the stations in the area. The air was gray, hazy and moist. I pulled my muffler from my purse and wound it around my neck, shivering. I bought instant ramen, eggs, scallions, two carrots, a stick of celery and, at the liquor store, two large bottles of Kirin beer. By the time I got back to Jinbocho it was pitch dark, the front door of the bookstore was locked and there was no one there. I unlocked the door, entered the store, locked the door again, put the food and beer down and wrote a note for Eric that I pasted to the front door with scotch tape telling him to call up to me from the front of the store. At fifteen to six I was standing by my window looking down on the street. It felt like every minute was lasting an hour. Did Eric have some bad news for me?

Then the two Americans appeared in front of the shop. They looked up at my window. I quickly stepped back. I don't think they saw me. I was afraid to get close to the window and look down again. But at six I heard Eric calling to me from the front of the store.

—Karen! Karen!

I rushed downstairs, opened the front door, pulled him in, locked the door and fell into his arms.

—Why didn't you call me?

Eric had been sent somewhere, he wouldn't tell me where.

—All I can say is, it was in Japan.

—Some sort of training mission?

—Look, I feel really funny talking about this now. Do you really want to know?

We were standing at the bottom of the stairs that went up to my room.

—No, I'd rather you kissed me.

I led him up the stairs and opened my door. I had left my futon out in the morning. In fact, I had grown tired of folding it, layer by layer, and storing it on the shelf in the sliding-door closet.

I locked the door behind us. Eric pointed to the corner by the window.

—I see Hiro's helmet and stick are still here. How long's he going to keep those things here?

—I don't know. But it doesn't faze me. Kiss me.

I put my hands on his hips.

—Listen, Karen, are you sure we should be doing this?

—Yes. I'm sure. If I weren't sure, I wouldn't be doing it, that's for sure.

—What would your daddy say if he could see you now?

—I don't care.

—You would've cared a month ago.

—So?

He started to unbutton his shirt.

—Don't you want to do mine first?

—Uh, yeah, suppose so.

He unbuttoned my blouse and then unbuttoned his shirt. I turned my back to him.

—What'd you do that for?

—Undo my bra.

He lifted my loose blouse up by the hem and I let it slip off me. He seemed to be fumbling with the hooks of my bra.

—I'm all butterfingers. Must be nervous.

—Let me help you.

I unhooked the six hooks on my bra, dropped it to the floor and turned toward him.

—Jesus, Jesus.

—I thought you had been with a woman before.

—No, that was my brother. Me? Not really.

—Do you want to get into the futon?

I laid down on my side in the futon. Eric took off his pants and laid down facing me. He brought the futon completely over our heads and we both shivered from head to toe.

—It's goddamn freezing here.

—I know. I should get an electric blanket, but I can't afford one yet. Maybe after Christmas, when the sales are ... ooh, that's tickling me ... on.

He sat up, lifting the cover down to our shoulders.

—Okay, well why don't we wait till after Christmas then.

—Eric!

—Just kidding, baby.

We both laughed. He kissed me, slipping his tongue into my mouth and putting his hand over my breasts.

—Jesus, you are so beautiful. I'm sorry.

—Sorry, why?

—No, it's just that ... I've not, I've not had so much, uh, experience before, I mean, you know. Just one girl, really, a black girl, my second cousin Irma, oh, by marriage so it's okay. But it really didn't go, I mean, we didn't actually ... I mean, nothin' happened.

—You didn't go all the way?

—Yeah. No. Well, let's just say I went all the way by myself before she could get ... involved.

—So, you're a virgin.

—Guess so.

—Then that makes two of us.

He sat up.

—Look, baby, I really don't think this is such a good idea. We'll do it and you'll hold it against me for the rest of your life. Hey, your husband will ask, so, how did you lose your virginity, and you'll say, well sweetie-pie, there was this big black guy who ... who ...

—Shut up. How do you know who my husband's going to be? Besides, that's a long time from now. So, how was it?

—How was what?

—The first time, with Irma.

—Well, a bit of a fizzle, actually, like a sparkler that flares up and sort of goes out pretty much right away. It's like the fourth of July lasted only ten seconds. I don't know what Irma thought, but for me it was game over in two shakes of a lamb's tail, literally, I mean, before anyone even got to first base. I mean, she never even left the plate!

We both burst out laughing.

You want me to go on with this, don't you, daddy? I know you like this sort of thing. You want to hear everything that happened to your little blueberry girl, don't you? All the gory details. You'll lap it up. Not only Meiko Uehara, but Myra, Myra Moskowitz too. My friend from Lake Arrowhead summer camp. You remember Myra, sure you do! I was at this very hospital visiting mom the first time she got cancer. You were alone with Myra in the house. Remember the venetian blinds? That's what clinched it. I didn't believe her at first when she told me. I thought she was making the whole story up. But when the same thing happened to Mieko, it sort of clicked. Two similar stories by two girls who don't know each other, not very likely, eh, daddy? But that's all water under the bridge with you, isn't it. You would never have told me. How could you? I heard it from the both of them, the same story. So, you see, I want to tell you my story now too. Maybe it sort of cancels out yours. There's no way I'm going to let you get away without absorbing it all. Forced entry into your brain, daddy. You know all about that, don't you. Oh, I bet you wish you could move your hand now! You'd grab my arm, wouldn't you. You'd say, "Stop telling me these revolting things. And stop lying about what I did or didn't do to your friends." But you can't move a muscle, daddy, not a single muscle. You're the most pathetic weakling on Muscle Beach now. You've been reduced to being a 98-pound weakling. You've been reduced to next to nothing. So just lie there for once and take it like a man.

Eric started kissing me again, passionately, his beautiful black eyes closed and his silk hands coursing everywhere on my body, over my breasts, down my belly and between my legs. He took off his underpants and I took off mine. I looked down and watched his penis go into me. My skin looked gray under the cover, a shadow of his. His body was so warm, daddy, and it covered mine and I put my hands on his hips and he kept pulling almost all the way out of me then pushing back in over and over again and his fingers were pinching my nipples and he didn't stop kissing me all the while until he breathed over my face and lay motionless on top of me. Then he lifted his head up and he was smiling the most beautiful smile I've ever seen. Then he whispered …

—Thank you. Thank you.

—Thank you, sweetheart.

—Am I your sweetheart, baby?

—Do you want to be?

—Forever. At least forever, baby.

We pulled the cover over ourselves again, clung to each other and started kissing in the pitch dark. I pressed myself against him and though there was a hazy crack of light coming in from where the cover had slid to the side, I couldn't see where his skin ended and mine began.

There were two knocks at the door and Dr. Chuck Price, the intern, came back in.

—How're we doing? I've been meaning to stop in again but tonight's just been crazy. Everybody wants a piece of me.

(He's fiddling about with your tubes, daddy, can you feel it? You can move for him, daddy, it's safe.)

—Any signs?

—No, nothing. He's just the same.

—Breathing difficulties?

—No, uh, none.

—You are so heroic to stay up with him. Don't you have a boyfriend or something to go back to?

—No.

—That's unbelievable.

He pulled a bridge chair up beside me and put his hands on the arm of my chair.

—Nice dress.

—Thank you.

—Is that Bullocks?

—Pardon?

—From Bullocks on Wilshire Boulevard. My mom shops there.

—I don't know where it was bought.

—Ah, a gift from a lover boy, perhaps.

—My father. He gave it to me.

He slid his hand along the arm of the chair and rested it on my knee.

—You are a gorgeous little girl. Did anybody ever tell you that?

I lifted his hand off my knee.

—Sorry, I just meant to be gallant, kind, you know.

—Yeah, I know.

It's a real pity that you couldn't see what happened next, daddy. You would've appreciated it. He grabbed me by the shoulders, twisted me around in my chair and kissed me on the mouth. He applied so much pressure that I had a hard time wrenching my lips off of his.

—Oh my God. You are so gorgeous, so so gorgeous.

—Leave me alone! Just you leave me alone!

He stretched out his hand toward me. I pushed it aside with my forearm.

—Don't be like that.

He stood up and pulled my head in against his pelvis.

—Come here. I'm so excited. Can you feel me? I've just got undies under my smock.

—Let go of my head!

—Not for a minute. Just a minute. Oh my God, I'm so hard. I can feel your cheek against me. Oh God.

He was gripping the back of my head with great force, pushing my face up and down against the front of his smock.

—Let go of me!

—Just one more minute. Just ... just ...

He twisted my head around in his grip until my mouth was pressed hard against his penis. He looked down at me, then up to the ceiling, his jaw dropped, his breathing getting heavier and heavier. I stretched both my hands up and scratched the sides of his neck as hard as I could. He immediately let go of my head and covered the scratches with his palms.

—I'm bleeding. Damn you, you made me bleed.

I stood and went around to the other side of the bed. You see, daddy, you were shielding me from an attack. You're my savior. I'm relying on you, daddy, I'm putting myself in your hands now.

—Okay, okay. You don't need to get so uptight about it.

—Get out. Get out of this room!

—Jesus. You don't need to react that way. Forget it, all right? Just forget it. Christ Almighty, you've hurt me. You've really hurt me. Get fucked, will you!

He walked out, rubbing his palms on the sides of his smock and slamming the door behind him. I'm looking down on you now, daddy, and thinking. Maybe, just maybe, you opened your eyes and saw what happened. If you had, it would've been worth it. It would have been worth it to have you witness that. Maybe it would have got your blood boiling. Maybe you would have mustered strength from some unknown source, from disgust or indignation or fury, managed to rip the tubes out of your body like some dinosaur, like Godzilla breaking out of his chains and lunging forward. You would've wrapped those tubes around the neck of the little intern in his thin green smock, wouldn't you have. What a spectacle that would be, the indignant father taking revenge for his daughter's honor, worthy of an opera, daddy, the father bent on strangling the villain about to defile his innocent daughter. Rigoletto played out in a hospital ward in modern-day Los Angeles! You've witnessed the first act and what are you going to do about it, eh? You going to lash back at the man who lays a hand on your daughter's flesh whether she likes it there or not? You going to jump out of bed the next time the little green intern comes back in, give him a good piece of your mind, punch him in the face and have him sacked later for daring to lay so much as a finger on your daughter? The intern will say, "I was just being friendly, only flirting, making a pass, that's all. She's exaggerating. She's blown it all out of proportion. It wasn't serious. Forget it." Then you'll shake hands with him and assure him, "Yes, it happens. Just make certain you don't do it again with my daughter." "Oh, I wouldn't dream of it, Dr. Rogers, wouldn't dream of it." You'll have a bond with the man after that, a special tie, man to man, stick together through thick and thin, after all, it's only natural, these things happen, men do that sort of thing, think nothing of it and, most of all, forget it. Yes, they do do that sort of thing. I know. They do. Come to think of it, Eric did it to me, daddy. I wanted him to, but that really doesn't matter to you, does it. I wanted him inside me, I wanted his body on top of mine, I wanted to feel his hips moving up and down over me, I wanted his big lips on mine. He made love to me five times that night, yep, he kept waking me up and I said, "Not again!" but he said he loved me and that we were going to be together for the longest longest time.

At ten the next morning there was a knock on my door. The store would have just opened and I expected it to be Nakano-san, even though I was off that day. Instead it was Hiro, looking completely bushed.

—We're just having breakfast, Hiro. I've got ramen with scrambled egg and scallions in it.

—No thanks, I'm not hungry. But can I come inside?

—Sure.

—Hi Hiro.

—Oh, Eric.

He lowered his gaze to the floor but otherwise did not seem surprised by seeing Eric in my room in the morning.

—Are you sure? What about a cup of coffee? I've got Nescafe.

—Thank you. Yes, I will have it.

Hiro told us that Emi had been arrested the night before at Haneda Airport.

—She was taking photographs around the fence, and policemen surrounded her. They led her to the police station at Kamata and questioned her for six hours, then they said she could make a phone call so she made the phone call to me. So I woke up and went to the police station, it was about three o'clock, and they questioned me too, but just the usual things like who my parents and brothers and sisters are, where I lived for five years before now and things like that. But they were questioning Emi in the room beside the room I was in, and I could hear, and it was awful, really awful. They wanted me to hear her. They were screaming at her and telling her she was a criminal against Japan and that she was not a real Japanese. They did not let her sleep all night and then they said we could go, so we went to my room and then she fell asleep and I came here to see my uncle.

—Here's your coffee, Hiro.

—Thank you.

—Should I put sugar in it for you?

—Yes please. Thank you. Can I sleep here only for a few hours? Then I will speak with my uncle.

I exchanged glances with Eric.

—Of course you can. But I have only those sheets. Is that okay?

—That is no problem for me. Thank you, Eric.

—Don't thank me, Hiro. It's no skin off my back. Thank Karen.

Hiro finished his coffee, folded his arms on the table and rested his head on them.

—You've been through a lot, Hiro.

Hiro raised his head.

—What? Oh no, not so much. Emi has worse. She is our leader. Remember when you were at Golden-gai in Shinjuku?

—Yes. But how do you know …

—Emi saw you. She saw you walking. That was a meeting. Emi is so smart. The police know this. They are waiting to crush us. I am not so strong as Emi.

—Yes you are, Hiro. You're very strong.

—Thank you, Karen, but it is not so. I will sleep here. Can I leave my helmet and *gevabo* here? I cannot take them back to my room. The police may come there at any time now that they know where I live, even when I am not there. I brought all my *bira* to here, to my uncle. How do you say that?

—*Bira*? Flyers.

—Oh, I cannot pronounce that, Karen-san. It would sound like "fryers." So I say *bira*.

—What are they for?

—They are for Kyushu, Eric. In January. We are going. Emi is going. You know the Enterprise?

Eric chuckled.

—Do I know it? I've been on it, man.

—Well, it is coming to Sasebo port in Kyushu. We are going to demonstrate and stop it. Enterprise is nuclear, I mean, it has nuclear power. This is very bad. This is the same power that destroyed Hiroshima and Nagasaki. So we must stop it. Now I must sleep. I am very sleepy. Please tell my uncle that I will come down later. Thank you.

He laid down in the futon, covered himself, removed his pants and shirt, and within a minute was dead to the world.

Eric and I went downstairs where Nakano-san was chatting to a Western woman dressed in jeans, a white blouse, a long woollen jacket and tall black leather boots.

—I'm looking for something by Lafcadio Hearn.

—Yes, we have much by him, madam. We have catalogued him under his adopted Japanese name, Koizumi Yakumo. Do you know he was once in this bookstore? It is many many years ago, in my grandfather's time.

As Nakano-san was speaking to her, he smiled and bowed to us as we left the bookstore.

—*Itterasshai.* (Come back soon.)

I smiled back and said …

—*Itte kimasu.* (I'll be back, goodbye.)

—I don't believe it.

—What, Eric?

—You have picked up the lingo so amazingly. You amaze me, baby.

—What do you think I do every night when you don't phone me, huh?

—Go to nightclubs in Roppongi and dance with American soldiers?

—Eric, I do not. I have not once gone out at night without …

—I know, baby, I know. I'm joshing. Can't you take a joke?

He reached for my hand, but I pulled it back as if given an electric shock.

—Can't hold hands in public. This is Japan, remember.

—Oh, boy, you're destroying me with all this assimilation.

I pecked him on the jaw.

—Just joshing. Can't you take a joke?

We walked along the main street at Jinbocho until we came to Kudanshita.

—I want to go to Yasukuni Shrine, Eric.

—I've heard of it. What is it?

—It's right here. See that big red, I mean, those two big pillars with the, like, crossbeam on top?

—Yeah.

—That's it. It's where Japanese people go to pray for soldiers who died in the war, I mean, in all wars they've been in.

We walked between the pillars down the wide path that led to the shrine. Eric suddenly stopped.

—You know how I said I'd been away?

—Yes. On your hush-hush mission.

—It's no joke. May as well tell you. We were taken to Okinawa and we were sworn to secrecy, but I know I can tell you.

—I want you to tell me everything that happens to you, sweetheart.

I held his arm against my side.

—We got bases there, like, the main ones for the bombers that go to Vietnam and they got these drums of stuff … it's in these orange drums.

He paused and looked up at the branches of the trees that lined the path. A gust of wind sent a swirl of dust in the air and dead leaves came fluttering to the ground by our feet.

—What stuff? What kind of stuff?

—I don't know. Some kind of gas maybe or something. No one would say a thing about it. But one of my buddies who's been, you know, in Vietnam, said they drop this stuff all over where the Viet Cong are and it gets rid of all the leaves so they can't hide anymore. Since they have nowhere to hide we can see them and kind of flush them out, I mean, bring them into the open where we can shoot at them. But my buddies say that the stuff is like poison too and that when you breathe it in or get it on you, you get the shakes and you chuck up and you gotta be, you know, in some cases, you gotta be flown home because you've had it. So now you know where I was.

—That's, I mean … you can't be involved in that.

—Jesus, Karen, can't be involved? What do you think this war is, cowboys and Indians, like? Man, it's huge, it's a massacre anyway you look at it, and I'm involved in it, like deep shit involved, whether I like it or not.

He walked ahead of me and sat on a bench in front of an old white stone building. I sat beside him.

—I'm sorry, Eric. I didn't mean it that way. What I meant was, I don't want you getting yourself injured like that. I don't want you to get hurt.

—What about dropping all that stuff on those poor people, huh? They're just farmers out there and they're in their own country. It's not our country. Do you think we'd sit back and take it if they dropped that stuff on us, I mean, like, on your precious Pali High?

—There's no need to blame this on me, Eric. I'm not dropping that stuff on anybody.

—Then who is, Karen? Who is? The man you say you love sure is, at least, he's going to. Why do you think they sent me to Okinawa, for my health or something?

He stood up and walked into the building. I followed him. It was a small museum dedicated to war. Only a few of the exhibits had English explanations, so we just walked from room to room of uniforms, swords and photographs and things until Eric stopped in front of one display window.

—Look. It's a letter from a kamikaze pilot to his mother. They've translated it. It says he wants her to be proud of him, that he's doing it for the Emperor. He doesn't mind dying and he doesn't want her to be sad. Jesus, I don't think I could write a letter like that to my dad. I'd be scared shitless. How could he be so calm when he knows, I mean, he actually knows that in a few hours from then he's going to be dead? They only gave them fuel for a one-way trip.

—That was a terrible thing to ask them to do.

—Yeah, terrible. But what's the difference? What's the difference between them and us?

—You don't know for sure that you're going to die.

—No, maybe not for sure. But you know that you're going to kill some innocent people for sure. How do you live with that for the rest of your life?

An old Japanese man walked into the room. When he saw us, a tall Negro man and a blond white woman, standing in front of the display window, he stopped, rested his hands on his cane and stared at us. I bowed to him. Eric took my arm.

—Let's go.

We passed the old man as we walked out of the room. He just stood there like a statue, resting on his cane and staring through the glass at the photograph of the pilot who wrote the letter to his mother.

We walked for over an hour, stopped in at a tempura restaurant for lunch and returned to the bookstore just before three. Nakano-san was alone behind the counter.

—Hiromasa has gone. He told me to be very thankful to you.

—Is he going to be all right?

—Yes he is, Karen-san. I am helping him. My brother died because of the war so I must.

—Oh, I am so sorry to hear that.

—Yes. It was after the war. He came back from New Guinea and Manila with many diseases. He married his sweetheart and became a father to Hiromasa, but then he suddenly got so weak and died, like a thin little candle going out. I am guilty because I did not go to the war. I was too short. Even at the end of the war I was still too short, you know, even when they made the soldier height lower as the war went on. I feel guilty that my brother died and I did not die. So I must look after Hiromasa and protect him.

I took Eric up to my room. Hiro had put the futon in the closet and washed all the dishes.

—I better be getting back. I promised my buddies I'd see them tonight.

—Does anybody on the base know about us?

—What? Of course not. You're my biggest secret, baby.

—Not forever, I hope.

—Are you having me on again? No way. When the time comes I'm going to shout it out to the whole damn world, starting with my father, blast it from the highest hilltops.

—Me too, sweetheart. I'm going to tell the world too.

—Starting with your father?

—Hmmm. No, I'll tell Jeff first.

—Your brother.

—Yes. We were very close. Once.

—Aren't you still close?

—I think so. Now kiss me before you go.

He put his arms around me and lifted me up, kissing my mouth and cheeks and nose and eyes.

—I love you to bits, baby.

—I love you, Eric. I really really love you.

After Eric left I watched the shop for an hour while Nakano-san went out, even though I was not officially working that day, and spent the evening studying Japanese. I pulled the futon down from the closet, laid it on the tatami, layer by layer, took a shower, got into my pyjamas, slipped under the covers and whispered to myself, "*Oyasumi nasai*, Eric. Good night, sweetheart."

I slept for nine hours without waking up once, dreaming that Eric and I were at Disneyland together. We went from Adventureland to Tomorrowland and to Fantasyland, but each time we got inside an entrance the scene changed to a warzone and we ran out like crazy. Eric was screaming. The next thing I knew we were in the Tunnel of Love and Eric was holding and kissing me, but when we sailed out of the tunnel Eric was gone. I stood up alone in the little boat and looked around frantically. On each side of the river there was a jungle, but the trees had no leaves on them and there were none on the ground either. There were lots of dead bodies strewn about, some of them without arms and legs. I jumped out of the boat. Then I was surrounded by piled-up dead bodies, so many that I couldn't see over them.

It was hard to find a place to put my feet. I was wearing long black leather boots like the ones the Western lady wore in the bookstore, and I had to walk around as carefully as I could so as not to step on corpses. The corpses were Asian and American, and a lot of the American ones were Negroes. I knelt down and lifted the head of the Negro corpses by the chin but none of them was Eric. I screamed his name. ERIC! Then I was in a rice paddy encircled by Vietnamese farmers. I screamed his name again. ERIC! ERIC! I caught sight of Eric standing behind a small group of farmers in a rice paddy. He beckoned to me with his finger and I could hear him saying, "Come, Karen, it's okay. It's not dangerous at all. These are really nice people. They don't hate us." But as I started to walk through the paddy my boots sank down deeper and deeper into the mud. Before I was even halfway to Eric I was up to my knees in mud and I couldn't move my legs at all. I called out to him again. ERIC! ERIC! I wanted him to come and get me, to pull me out of the mud. I looked around me. It was nighttime and there was no one at all in sight, not even Eric. I don't know how many times I called out his name or whether I was still doing it when I woke up in the morning. I felt incredibly groggy. I wept and said to myself, "I need you, I need you so much." For a moment I had no idea at all where I was. I had no idea what would happen to me. I shivered all over, and my body wouldn't stop shaking. I would have to get that electric blanket if I was going to survive the winter. And I would have to somehow make contact with Jeff to tell him about how my life had turned around. And I would have to find out about his.

The next day two men came into the bookstore and asked to speak to Nakano-san. I bowed to them at the counter.

—*Chotto matte kudasai.* (Please wait a minute.)

I went into the little storeroom behind the counter where

Nakano-san was sorting new stock. He dropped what he was doing and came out. Though my Japanese was improving I could not follow the conversation between Nakano-san and the two men. But I could tell that they were speaking in very polite language to him. After they left, he called me into the storeroom.

—Those men are from the police. They are policemen in ordinary clothes.

—Why did they come here?

—Hmm, yes. I am not sure. Maybe they follow Hiromasa, that is possible. They wanted to know if suspicious people were coming into the bookstore.

—Suspicious? What do you mean?

—Yes. I am not sure. Maybe radical students. They asked about you too.

—About me? Why?

—I think no reason. They just saw you here. I said that you were a student helping me by doing *arubaito*.

—What's that?

—It's part-time work. I said that my English was not so good and I needed you to help. It is always a good thing to be humble with Japanese people. They believe you are good when you are humble, even if it is an act. But then they asked about the upstairs room.

—How did they know about that?

—I think they saw the window from the street. They could know from official files kept at the ward office too that there is a room above the bookstore.

—What did you say?

—I said that it is unused. I did not want to say that you lived there because you are not registered as an alien to live there. This would have caused a problem.

—Thank you.

—Not at all. Then they asked if they could see the room.

—Oh my gosh.

—I immediately said, "Yes, of course," and began to take the key off my key ring.

—Why did you do that? If they went up there they would have seen that someone was living there.

—Yes, I know. But because I was so quick to let them, they said, "Well, it won't be necessary today." Then they left.

—Yes, I saw them leave. They bowed to me politely.

—They are very polite. That is their way. In Japan when people are too polite, sometimes you should be afraid of them.

I would have to get rid of Hiro's helmet and stick just in case the police returned to inspect my room. Nakano-san could always say that I sometimes stayed over when working late. But if they saw the helmet and stick they would know there was some connection with radical students. They would soon connect Nakano-san to Hiro, his nephew, and then to Emi. Who knows, they might even start investigating me and find out that I hadn't been living on the base, which was the address on my alien registration card, and that I hadn't been attending classes. They might even link me with Eric and report him to the American military police. Of all things I couldn't let that happen.

That night I wrote a letter to Jeff in Nepal, telling him about how I had moved off the base and had met Eric. But I didn't mention that Eric was a Negro. Not that I thought Jeff would object. He would probably say, "That's really cool" or something like that. I don't know. I just left it out. But I told him absolutely everything else, even that I was in love with Eric and that we had spent a night together. I got all teary again while writing the letter and had to blot out the teardrops on the paper with the side of my hand. At the end I wrote …

I miss you so much, Jeff, I really really miss you. It's as if we haven't really had time to talk ever until now. I want to see you so much. I know that when we meet next time we'll just talk and talk and hug and everything will be all right. Everything that happened at home in the past is going to be all right.
Your loving sister,
Karen

Just after I finished writing the letter I heard the phone ringing downstairs. No one called the store after hours. It had to be Eric. I told him to let it ring and ring until I had enough time to get downstairs to answer it. I raced down the stairs and picked up the receiver.

—Hello. Hello?

There was no sound at the other end of the line.

—Hello? Eric? Eric, is that …

Whoever it was, the person hung up. I waited for a moment by the phone, but it didn't ring again. It was freezing in the corridor where the phone was, and I was wearing only a thin sweater over my pyjamas. There was a kerosene heater in my room and one in the store, but no heater in the corridor. I waited. The phone didn't ring. I was halfway up the stairs when it rang again. I paused for a few seconds on the stairs, then raced down. I didn't say anything at first. After a long pause I heard Eric's voice.

—Hello? Karen? Are you there? Hello?

—Eric, Eric.

—It's me, baby. I tried you a few minutes ago but I couldn't hear anything, and then I couldn't get through.

—Oh, I miss you so much.

—Me too, me too. But I had to be here tonight. Two of the boys are off to Saigon tomorrow and we had a kind of, well I don't want to call it a farewell party, a kind of, uh, going away thingo here for them.

—Can I see you during the week? I don't want to wait until next weekend. I can see you on Saturday all day and night too, though.

—I don't know. It's really hard for me to get away from the base during the week. Let's make it after Christmas for sure. How's that?

—I could come there to see you.

—Well, yeah, but that's not such a good idea, baby.

—Why not? You could say I was just a friend.

—White girl, black guy. Friends? People will talk. How does that look?

—Talk? I could care less. I'll come one evening and meet you off the base at one of those places they've got there.

—They're crawling with servicemen, baby.

There was a long silence.

—Karen? Karen?

—I'm here.

—Once we get up to after Christmas, I'll get more time off and I can stay with you, maybe even for a few days together. Would you like that?

—Yes.

—Karen?

—Yes.

—Come the new year, I might have to take another one of those trips for a while.

—Where?

—I can't say where, baby. But I will be coming back for sure.

—I may move out for a few days or so on Christmas Eve.

—Move out?

—Yes. Jeanette Rush, that's the daughter from the people I stayed with on the base, she and I met and she said that her parents wanted to invite me for Christmas to come back because they wanted me to have an American Christmas, and also because they'd promised my dad and stuff that I'd be there.

—Okay. We'll work it all out, baby. You just cuddle up tonight and I'll get in touch sometime during the week as soon as I can.

—Okay. Goodnight.

—Oh-ya-sue-me, isn't that right?

—Yes. But you've got a horrible American accent.

—Why sure, baby, I'm a red-blooded American, that's why. Goodnight.

I held the receiver against my ear for about half a minute after he hung up, replaced it on the hook, climbed the stairs and returned to my room. I addressed the letter to Jeff in care of the temple he was staying at in Kathmandu, turned off my heater, laid down in my futon and, before I knew it, had fallen fast asleep.

I was determined to see Eric that week, even if only for a few minutes or an hour. So when he called me on Tuesday night I said I was going to Camp Zama to see him on Wednesday. He was reluctant, but he agreed to meet me at 6:30 at a bar called "The A Train" not far from the base. I asked Nakano-san if I could leave the bookstore at 4:30, walked to Suidobashi and took the Chuo Line to Shinjuku, where I changed to the Odakyu Line. When I arrived at Sobudai Station luckily there was a bus about to go in the direction of the base. I asked a young Japanese man for directions to "The A Train," and when I got there at 6:20, Eric was already sitting alone at a table. He stood up and waved when I walked in. The only other people there were two American men in shiny leather jackets hunched over the bar.

—Hi.

—Hi.

—Have trouble finding this place?

—None at all. Everybody is very nice.

—Want a beer?

—Yes, thank you. I'm pretty hungry too.

—Okay. Hey, Taka-san. Two Millers and a packet of beer nuts over here.

The middle-aged Japanese bartender, who was completely bald but had a jet-black goatee, was polishing glasses.

—Coming up, Eric-san.

—So, what's new?

—I wrote a letter to my brother.

—At least you've got a brother to write a letter to. Sorry. Don't know where that came from.

—No, it's okay.

I took his hand and held it up to my cheek. Eric looked around.

—Not here, baby.

I let go of his hand.

—Right. Just friends.

—No, geez, I don't mean it that way. It's just that, you know, the guys here, I mean ...

—Uh-huh. I get it.

—No, I can see that you don't. Once this is all over I won't care who says what, you know that.

—Once this is all over. What is "this"?

—This, baby. This place, this situation, this war and everything.

The bartender walked up to our table with two opened bottles of beer, two glasses and a bowl full of nuts.

—Thanks, Taka-san.

—Should I play that song for you and your friend?

Eric looked down at the table. He was clearly embarrassed.

—What song, Eric?

—Oh, Eric started to ask me a couple of weeks ago, "Please please Taka-san, play a song for me." He told me the title, and I have it in my collection. I'll play it. I think it might be about you.

Eric put his face in his hands. I poured our beers and popped a few nuts into my mouth. Then I heard "Earth Angel" coming from speakers perched on either side of the bar.

—Look, baby, I don't know what he's talking about. It's an old song, a really old song.

I looked toward the bar. Taka-san was pointing to us. The two men sitting at the bar turned around. I got a terrible fright. For a split second I thought they were the two Americans who had come into the bookstore, because one of them was much taller than the other. But they weren't. One of the men gave Eric the thumbs up sign. They both turned back toward Taka-san, hunched their backs and put their heads together, whispering to each other.

—They know nothing, absolutely nothing.

—What do you mean? Those guys at the bar?

—No. I mean, the guys at the base. They grow up in some little suburb in Atlanta or Cleveland or, or somewhere, I don't know, downtown in a city, and, you know, not all of them, I mean especially the white guys, not all of them are underprivileged. They should know better. When they're kids, they're in their little Norman Rockwell world, in their little classrooms where the girls wear pigtails and the teachers stand in front of a map of the United States and tell them fairy tales about democracy and town meetings in Vermont or somewhere, I don't know, and freedom, you know, everybody being free, everybody counting, but no one tells them about the nooses, the nooses that got put around the necks of black people and about people around the world who don't want to be, you know, don't, I mean …

—Eric, where is this all coming from all of a sudden? I

thought you wanted to see me.

—Shit, I flubbed up again. Yeah, it was always my brother Gordon who was the articulate one in the family. Look, I don't know, I just got so damn upset when my buddies shipped out on Monday, I guess. I mean, where are they going to be spending Christmas, huh? Up to their shins in stinking mud and not knowing who they're shooting at or why, or who's shooting back at them? Look, baby, this has turned out all wrong. I just wanted to see you so badly. And now, I don't know why I … why I …

—You're upset, sweetheart, that's why. Your buddies have gone. Maybe you're worried that you'll be sent too. You won't be, will you?

He leaned toward me.

—Don't know. But I do know that they're sending some of us on another trip first thing in the new year like I said, but don't ask where. I won't even know for sure myself until the morning we leave. But I'll be back.

—You've got to me promise me that you won't go anywhere you won't come back from.

He chuckled under his breath.

—Yeah. Right. It always happens to the other guy, doesn't it. God has something different in store for you. Everyone thinks that. He's sitting up there in the control tower watching all the planes coming in and taking off. Then, as it happens, you know, chance or whatever you want to call it, a plane takes off, careens to one side and, boom, it's all over in a big flash. Everyone back home watches it on the six o'clock news, they, I don't know, kind of relive it in their living rooms, just like they relive pictures of all those hamlets that get burnt to the ground in towns no one ever heard of and look so remote from their lives at home. But what if it's you on that plane or someone you love? What if you're the one setting fire to those hamlets? It's not the same, and whether it's fluke or fate or a combination of the two, after a while you come to realize that your egg is in their basket and someone else is carrying it, and when the whole thing gets dropped or smashed against a wall or crushed by a tank, you go with it. You're just a thin little shell, that's what your life is, and you can't pretend that your fate isn't right there in the same spot with anyone else's. That old man in the control tower, that great white father, he just sits there and looks down. And I don't care what anyone says, he couldn't've stopped it, otherwise he would've. It's even beyond his control. It's beyond the control of all of us, baby. No one can do a goddamn thing about it.

"Earth Angel" had finished and the bar was filling up with Americans and their Japanese girlfriends. Eric and I left. We strolled over to the perimeter fence of the base. Several helicopters were hovering overhead waiting to land, and the whirring of their blades was so loud that my eardrums shuddered. Jeeps and black sedans were screeching past behind us. Big yellow lights by the helicopter pads shone onto Eric's face, and I could see that something was still deeply troubling him, that he was not himself.

I took his hands and put them over my breasts.

—Not here, baby!

—It's okay. No one can see us. Kiss me.

He bent down and kissed me, leaving his hands on my breasts.

—I've got to get back now. It'll take like two hours for me to get back now, so.

—Sure. I'm so, I mean, grateful that you came. But from now on I'm going to see you where you are. It's safer.

He kissed me again and walked me back to the station. I didn't tell him about the policemen who came into the bookstore. I felt then that it was too separated from him to matter.

On Saturday I went back to the Rushes' home in Tachikawa

for the first time in four weeks. When I arrived only Fran was home.

—Dad's working. He's always working. Mom's playing contract bridge. It's her new obsession. Canasta's old hat now, and only the Jewish women play Mahjong.

—So where's Jeannie?

—Oh, Jeannie's out again. It's getting so tedious. She'll be back for dinner though. Tomorrow's Christmas Eve, but mom is going to make one of her specialties tonight. Liver. Barf.

Fran stuck her tongue out and pretended to throw up.

—Wanna see my room?

—Sure.

We walked down the hall and up the stairs.

—Where's Kimiko?

—She went to visit her mother, because tomorrow is Sunday and that's the day she usually does, but she's going to be busy helping mom later get the Christmas dinner ready and things so she'll be back.

—Is she okay?

—Who? Mom?

—Kimiko.

—Dunno. Guess so. You'll be staying in your old room, Karen, so just drop your bag here.

Nothing had changed at all in my room, but after all it had only been a matter of weeks since I had lived in it. I guess my feeling so strange was a sign of how much I had changed in the short time since I left.

Fran called me into her room. Her shelves were lined with dolls. There must have been four or five dozen of them.

—I had all my Tammy dolls brought from L.A., you know, but I got some new ones since you were here, like this one, it's called "Grown Up Tammy." But this one is my prize beauty, it's "Colored Francie." It's the newest, and it's so neat and I'm the only girl on the base who has one right now. All the other girls' dolls are really dinky. Marsha has just two crummy dolls. Wanna hold her?

She handed me a chocolate-colored doll with long shiny black hair and a see-through sleeveless blouse over what looked like a bikini.

—Isn't she neat?

—Yes, but her features are a white girl's. Colored people don't generally look like this.

—So? It's only a doll. It is colored. That's its color.

She thrust her hand out. I gave her her doll back, and she laid it on its side on the bottom shelf.

—She's going to take a nap now.

Just then we heard someone come in the front door.

—Fran? You here?

—Yes, mom, upstairs!

Fran bolted out of the room and ran down the stairs.

—Karen's here. She just got here.

Fran's mother stood at the bottom of the stairs as I came down.

—My, my, it seems like a coon's age. How have you been?

—Fine, Mrs. Rush, thank you.

—Ben had to do one hell of a speech to the dean on your behalf, you know. Fortunately he's a dear friend. They're expecting you back in class sometime soon in the new year.

—I'll do my best.

—I know you will. It's not easy being young. You can ask Fran and Jeanette about that! Now, I've got a heap of groceries in the trunk. Can you girls activate some elbow grease and haul them in for me?

While Mrs. Rush was cooking I went to my room to have a nap. I don't remember falling asleep, but the first thing I knew

Fran was standing beside my bed shaking it.

—Gotta get up, Karen. Gotta get up. Shhh.

—What is it? What time is it?

—It's 5:30. But an awful thing has happened.

—Oh gosh, what is it?

Fran led me downstairs into the kitchen. Kimiko was sitting at the kitchen table. Her face was bright red and she was crying. Mrs. Rush was standing over her with her hands on her hips. Kimiko raised her head and, when she noticed me, she started to sob uncontrollably.

—No, Karen, leave her be. She has to pay for what she did. Ben'll be home soon and we'll all go into the den and have a powwow about what exactly we're going to do about this.

—Mom, can I have a Mounds?

—Not now, Fran, can't you see what's happening here? Besides, it'll ruin your dinner.

—Mom, when is Jeannie coming home?

—I don't know! She went to where Washington Heights used to be with that nice lieutenant, but she promised she'd be home by dinnertime.

—What happened, Mrs. Rush?

—What happened? See that big bowl for serving soup next to the sink?

—Yes.

—Can't you see it's broken right in two?

I nodded.

—Well, who do you think broke it?

Kimiko stopped sobbing and looked up to me.

—I did not break the bowl. The bowl was broken when I take it out.

—That bowl was not broken before! It's an heirloom, from my ancestors in England.

—Karen, it was broken. *Shinjite kudasai!*

—What did she say?

—She said, "Please believe me."

—Believe her? The last time we used that bowl I put it away myself. There wasn't so much as a crack in it.

—But maybe it was just old and …

—Karen, I don't think you realize. These people have to take responsibility for the things that they do. They can't just go, I mean, haywire or whatever or destroy things that are valuable to other people and wash their hands of it. We've seen enough of that with them.

—But she does say that she …

—Well my, my, perhaps you're the one who's become a little disoriented here.

The front door opened.

—Hello, honey, I'm back.

Mrs. Rush went into the hall.

—Good. Perhaps now we'll get to the bottom of this.

Ethel went to the front door. We could hear her telling her husband about the soup bowl. I walked up to Kimiko and put my hand on her shoulder. She immediately grabbed it with both hands and gripped it tightly. I looked to Fran.

—Don't look at me like that. I was upstairs playing with my dolls. I never touch those dishes anyway. That's her job.

Dr. Ben was standing in the kitchen door.

—I think we should all go into the den where we can discuss this calmly and rationally. Hello, Karen.

—Hello, Dr. Rush. Thank you for all the help with the dean.

He waved his hand in front of his face.

—That's nothing. Happy to do whatever I can for your father.

We all went to the den. Kimiko wouldn't let go of my hand.

—Sit down on the couch, Kimiko. No, Karen, you please sit over there. Where's Jeanette?

—Oh, she'll be home soon, honey.

—Good. Now, let's sort this out.

—That bowl was my only real treasure.

—I know, Ethel. Shh. You calm down too. It doesn't help matters. Now, Kimiko, I understand you're saying you didn't break the bowl.

—It was broken.

—She says it was broken when she opened the cupboard door.

—Karen, please. These people don't feel personally about things like we do. It's Christmas, and we won't hold back our forgiveness. It's bad to lie, Kimiko. *Uso da-me.* (Lie bad.)

—*Uso ja nai desu.*

—She says it's not a lie.

—Yes, I know, Karen. I speak Japanese. I've been in this country a lot longer than you have. There's no shame so long as she confesses up to what she did. You see, Karen, these people are ruled by shame. If Kimiko didn't break it, who did?

We all looked at each other. Ethel knelt in front of Kimiko.

—Listen, dear, you've been with us for two years or so now, haven't you, and we've taken you in. I am going to ask you only one more time. We are not cross and we are not angry with you. We will not ask you to pay for the bowl and we won't even ask your mother to pay for it either. But God is your witness, you must know that. He sees all. You have to own up to your actions before Him. Otherwise you'll never be able to face the future if you have to regret your past.

—I don't think she understands, Ethel.

—She understands. She understands a lot more than she lets on to.

—Listen, Kimiko. Stand up, please.

Kimiko stood up in front of the couch. She was not crying anymore. She stared at Dr. Ben. He took hold of both her hands, as if about to inspect her palms and fingers.

—The bowl isn't important. This isn't about a bowl. Listen,

I was a young doctor many years ago serving my country here in Japan. There was a war on in Korea and some prisoners were brought here. I worked beside many Japanese men. They were wonderful men, strong and honest. Together we questioned the Korean prisoners. We used Japanese people because the Koreans spoke Japanese then. Once we had captured a very evil Korean man. He had tortured men and killed women and children, Kimiko. But he wouldn't admit it to us.

—Look, honey, is this doing any good?

—Just be quiet, Ethel, and let me finish. This is important for her. It's related. As a last resort I gave him a shot to, you know, loosen him up, and he started to tell us all the terrible things that he did. The worst crime in life is not what you do but that you hold your tongue before others when the world smells sin on your breath.

Kimiko pulled her hands toward herself and turned her gaze to me, as if begging me to come to her defence. Dr. Ben threw me a glance, shook his head to silence me and looked Kimiko in the eye.

—Go to your room. *Anata no heya iku ima.* (Your room go now.)

Kimiko left the room, but not before looking straight at me again. I felt that I had let her down.

—Can I have that Mounds now, mom? I promise I'll eat my dinner.

—All right, Fran. Just go and eat it. Just go.

The front doorbell rang and Fran rushed out of the room.

—I'll get it.

We stood in silence in the den.

—It's Jeannie, mom! She's back!

I went into the hall. Jeanette threw her purse down next to the umbrella stand and dashed into the kitchen. Then we all heard a short but piercing scream.

—Who did this? Who DID this?!

When we got to the kitchen, Jeanette was sitting at the table looking down on the two halves of the broken bowl in front of her, pounding her fists on the formica tabletop.

—Who did this? Who did this? Who did this?

—Jeannie, Jeannie honey, shush. You'll muss up your hair.

Jeanette picked up one of the halves of the bowl and flung it against the refrigerator, smashing it to bits.

—Jeannie!

Dr. Ben sat next to her and put his arm around her.

—Shh, Jeannie, shh. What's the matter? We're all here now. Just pull yourself together.

She picked up the other half of the bowl and held it above her head.

—Daddy, stop her! Don't let her!

—Shut up, Fran. You go to your room now.

—No.

—I said you go to your room this instant!

Fran ran out of the kitchen and up the stairs.

Well, daddy, you see what goes on in this household that you sent me to? I felt like grabbing my bag and escaping there and then. There was still time for me to catch a train back to Shinjuku and Jinbocho. This is not my family, after all, is it? These are not my people, are they?

Dr. Ben stroked Jeanette's hair.

—Shh, my little girl, shh. Daddy's here now. Everything's just fine. Calm down. Calm down.

Jeanette lowered the piece of the bowl to the table. Dr. Ben took it from her and handed it to Ethel, who laid it in the sink.

—He hurt me, daddy, he hurt me.

—Shh. What? Who hurt you?

—Ben, she says she's hurt. Look at her, perhaps she's hurt.

—You stay out of this, Ethel. Now, what do you mean, Jeannie? Who hurt you?

—She was out with Lt. Crispin.

Jeanette pounded her fists on the tabletop, but Dr. Ben clamped his hands over them to restrain her.

—Stop it, Jeannie. Were you with John?

Jeanette stared blankly at the table.

—Jeannie, were you with John today?

She nodded.

—What did he do to you?

—He hurt me.

—Where?

—In the vagina.

—Oh my God.

—Ethel, stay out of this, will you?

—But Ben …

—I said, STAY OUT of this!

—Ben, you find out what happened.

—Will you shut up?! Jeannie, tell us in your own words. We are here to protect you, you know that.

There was a long silence before she spoke.

—John Crispin made me take my clothes off … in his room.

—I thought you went to Washington Heights, I mean, where it was.

—That's where he said he was going to take me. But then he said there was a movie at the club, but then when we got there it was closed. There was no movie and he said he had gotten the day wrong. I think he got the day wrong on purpose. So he asked me if I wanted to see his room, I mean, where he lives.

—You didn't have to go to his room, did you?

—I know. But I had been out with him a few times and he was always so nice, except for one time before.

—What do you mean he "made you" take your clothes off?

—He made me!

—Okay, okay. Shh. Shhhhh. Calm down. Did he push you down or something?

—Yes.

—Where? I don't see any bruises.

—He pushed me down!

Jeanette let out a loud high-pitch scream again. Ethel covered her ears, shaking her head violently from side to side.

—Ethel, we can't go on if you're going to go off the deep end here. Now, Jeannie, if he pushed you, wherever, there will be traces. Where did he grab you? Just point to where.

She pointed to both of her hips.

—Okay, okay. Let me see. I've seen this sort of thing before. Stand up, Jeannie. Now take your dress off.

—Look, I think I ought to leave.

—Karen, you're staying. It's fine. I promised your father. This'll be over in a minute. Now, take your dress off, Jeannie.

Jeanette lifted her dress over her head and draped it over the back of the chair.

—Where now? Here? Well, there's a bit of redness.

—Ben, your daughter has been raped!

—Now you just shut up, Ethel! Get out of this kitchen then, okay? Just get out.

But Ethel didn't budge. She looked petrified.

—We don't know for sure yet. There is a procedure to this sort of thing. Now, Jeannie, don't worry. Everything is going to be okay. Daddy promises.

—He made me take my clothes off.

—Okay. How did he make you?

—He said if I didn't do it, he was strong and he would do it himself. I was so scared, daddy.

—I know, I know. Shhh. What did he do next?

—He opened my legs with his hands. He took off his belt and tied my wrists with it. Here. Right here. Then he took off his pants and pulled my undies down.

—Go on.

—I can't, daddy.

—Shhh. It's all right. I promise.

—He forced his … thing … inside, to go inside me. It hurt, daddy.

—I know. Did he stay like that?

—I don't know. I got sick. I think I threw up. Daddy, it wasn't the first time. It happened before Thanksgiving too. But I stopped him then and he said he was sorry. I couldn't tell you, I just couldn't. I hate … I hate …

—Okay. Right. Ethel, go into the bathroom and get one of your tranquilizers from the medicine cabinet. John Crispin is well known here at Tachikawa. He's, uh, I mean, he's from a very good background, graduated West Point, if I recall correctly. I don't want to get your little sister upset by all this. Now, stop shivering. Karen, there's a travel rug in the living room. Would you please fetch it and bring it here?

I went to the living room and returned to the kitchen with the rug. He draped it over Jeanette's shoulders.

—Tomorrow's Christmas Eve. In a few days we're all going to Okinawa. You can even swim there at the end of December. You'll be "Gidget Goes Okinawan," how's that, eh? This'll all blow over but, rest assured, I'm going to phone Gen. Blain tomorrow, I don't care if it is Christmas, and tell him everything that transpired in Lt. Crispin's quarters. John's bound to be at church tomorrow too, he's there every Sunday, and I'll give him a good talking-to. It's awful, I know. But there's no war or anything going on here. These are peaceful circumstances. We've got to deal with it in the proper manner. We can't ignore it and we're not going to. John will own up, I can tell you that.

But, Jeannie, the first time isn't always what they make it out to be. It isn't like Peyton Place, you know. John will apologize, I give my word on that, and of course Karen wouldn't tell a soul, we can count on that, so it'll be our little family secret for a while and then it'll be all just past. Just past. You want to be a cheerleader, don't you, next year?

Jeanette nodded and rested her head on her father's shoulder, and the two of them slowly rocked back and forth as if they were on a boat. I left them in the kitchen. I told Ethel that I was too tired for any dinner. I went up to my room and shut the door.

I wanted you to hear the story, daddy, because I know it all sounds familiar, even the part about the belt and the wrists, though it might smack of a cheap novel too close to home, eh? And the rest, daddy, the rest … you'd know all about it too, wouldn't you? There you go again with those interrupted breaths … four … five … six seconds … and a deep gasp … then mouth wide open but nothing going in or out. I'm holding the call button in my hand, daddy. Should I buzz it? If I did, the little green man will come rushing in again. Would he make me take my blueberry dress off, daddy? Would he throw me onto the bed at your feet and force open my legs? Would he violate me right under your nose? Ah, no, I can't call him. He can't be trusted. Even you know that, daddy. But don't stop breathing like that, daddy, not yet. You've got to hear the best part. Come on, breathe, daddy, breathe. Ten seconds and no breathing … give it the old college try. Yes … yes! An enormous gasp of air … I can almost hear your lungs filling up like two bicycle tires … and back to normal again. You've done it, daddy. You've managed to survive until now.

I left the Rush home early Tuesday morning, the 26th of December. A few hours later they set off for Okinawa on their family holiday.

I arrived at the bookstore just before ten. Nakano-san unlocked the front door for me.

—Did you have a merry Christmas, Karen-san?

—Yes, thank you. And how about you, Nakano-san?

—Oh I am not a Christian so I was working. Many customers come in at this time of the year. By the way, someone came in and left this for you.

He handed me a small blank unsealed envelope.

—Thank you. I'll put my bag away and be right down.

I went up to my room, washed my face and hands and opened the envelope. Inside it was a small piece of paper.

Howdy, mystery girl
Who's Eric?

For a second I wondered who it could have been written by, but then I remembered. It must be those two Americans who came into the store and later stood in front of it looking up at my window. How stupid of me to have taped that note to Eric on the shop door! I could kick myself for writing his name on it. I crumpled up the piece of paper and gripped it in my fist until my knuckles turned white.

Eric phoned at lunchtime to say that his holiday was starting on Thursday and that he would be able to spend five days with me.

—... if you still want me to, that is.

—Yes, yes, come. I miss you so much.

We were together for those five days, daddy. I had to work from ten to four, Eric spent the time reading books borrowed from the store. I went upstairs every day for lunch. We made love and ate sushi that Eric bought from a shop down the street.

—Look, baby, this book is called "You Can't Go Home Again."

—Is it a biography, somebody's biography?

—Maybe. A kind of fictional autobiography. Thomas Wolfe wrote it. Boy, that dude could write! I've never seen so many adjectives strung together at once. It's like a locomotive with hundreds of cars behind it coming straight at you.

At night we avoided Roppongi. We didn't want to meet up with any Americans. We walked up and down almost all the little streets in Shibuya and Shinjuku. The shops were open till late with all the sales on. On one of the evenings I took Eric to Matsuzakaya Department Store on the Ginza and bought him a suit with money I'd saved up.

—What do I need a suit for in Japan?

—Just try it on. You need it for me. I want to see how you look in a suit.

He came out of the fitting room with his charcoal gray suit on and donned a hat from the hatstand nearby. I stood behind him as he stared at himself in the mirror.

—Well? Do I look like a Beverly Hills lawyer now?

—No. You look like Malcolm X.

He swivelled around and shook his head.

—That's just about the funniest thing I've ever heard. Me looking like Malcolm X? No way, baby, no way.

Sunday December 31st was our last night together. We stayed up till midnight, lying in my futon to bring in the new year together.

—I wonder what kind of a year it will be. Jesus, 1968. Can't believe it's already 1968.

—It's our year, Eric. Karen and Eric's year.

—Yeah, but there's one thing I didn't tell you.

I sat up, resting my head against the wall.

—What, sweetheart?

—I'm going to Vietnam.

—Oh no. No. No.

—But wait, baby, it's only for a week.

—What do you mean, for a week?

—It's just a, you know, kind of familiarization tour of the place. Saigon, Danang, Hue. I'm coming back, don't you worry about that. No sweat.

—They won't make you stay once you get there, will they?

—They can't do that. It's all set. But the bad thing is, well, once they send you over for these tours, it's a kind of warm-up for the real thing. They'll put us through a special training thingo at Zama and then you go for good.

He sat up next to me. It was only a few minutes before midnight.

—I don't want to go, Karen. You know that.

—It's so unfair.

—Yeah. Unfair all around. Me, my buddies, the Vietnamese we're going to rip to pieces. Everybody loses. What good is it all? What good?

Tears were rolling down Eric's cheeks. He put his head in my lap.

—There's another thing I didn't tell you. It's about my brother.

—Don't talk about him now. It'll only upset you more.

—No, I want to tell you. I can't keep things from you anymore. I want to start off 1968 with no lies. Those thugs who murdered my brother ...

—They were criminals.

—Yeah. I told you they were white. They weren't. That's not how it happened. The thugs were black. They broke into dad's store to rob us. Gordon shouted at them to leave and they stabbed him in the heart. Dad was out getting something, I don't know, gas or something. I lost my brother and for what? For no reason at all. There's no lesson in it. Nothing. No winners. So who're my people then, eh? Do those thugs have to be less guilty in my eyes because they were my people? I'm the one who had the Norman Rockwell upbringing, Karen. I'm the one who should've known better and gone to Canada or somewhere instead of ending up here. I missed the boat, baby. I missed it badly.

—Were they caught? The thugs?

—Oh yes. They were caught and sent to jail for a long time. They were addicts. Their own parents had got them hooked on drugs. Nobody wins. Nobody wins, Karen.

—Shh. I'm so sorry about your brother.

—Yeah.

We watched the hands of the clock over my desk without speaking.

—In two minutes it will be a new year, sweetheart.

I stroked his hair and wiped the tears from his cheeks.

—How does a guy find a place for himself in this world, baby? That's what I want to know.

—You will, Eric. I'll help you. Once you get back home, I'll help you. You could go back to Rutgers, to grad school or something. Study business administration and take over your dad's store. I'll work in it for you. I'll do whatever I have to do. My eggs are in your basket now.

I took his hand and placed it on my belly. The hands of the clock showed midnight, and we laid down again and hugged, clinging to each other.

—Go back home. Yeah, I'll go back home … in a big plastic bag. You can't go home again, isn't that right?

—Don't say that. Don't you say that! You are not going home that way. If they're going to send you to Vietnam to fight I'll get in touch with Hiro and Emi before and they can get you to Sweden. I'll join you there. I heard that in Sweden people don't even blink an eye when they see a black man with a white woman. We'll manage, Eric. We'll get through all this. We've got to believe that.

—You are so amazing, baby. I can't believe how amazing you are.

Eric left the next morning. I didn't hear from him for over a week. All the city's shops were closed during the first three days of the new year, and I spent them studying Japanese and walking the empty streets where Eric and I had been. The only place that was crowded with people was Yasukuni Shrine. I was lonelier than I had ever been in my life. But just thinking about Eric helped me cope. I was determined to find out how to get Eric out of Japan to a place where he would be safe. Even if it meant we could never go back to the United States, it was worth it.

The bookstore reopened on January 4th. When I came downstairs Nakano-san was already sitting behind the counter, drinking green tea. He stood up and bowed.

—*Akemashite omedeto gozaimasu.* (I wish you a happy New Year.)

—*Omedeto gozaimasu.* (Happy New Year.)

—Your Japanese is very proper, Karen-san.

—*Do itashimashite.* (Don't mention it.)

—Oh my goodness, you speak more polite Japanese than young Japanese people today. Today they are very, how do you say, direct? And they make terrible mistakes of grammar on their placards at demonstrations. Would you like a cup of tea?

—Tea? Yes, please. Thank you.

He poured hot water from a large thermos with a spout into a tiny teapot and jiggled the pot around for a few seconds.

—Here you are. This tea is from Uji in Kyoto. My wife's family is from Uji. They have the best tea in Japan.

I took the teacup from the tray he was holding.

—May I ask you a question, Nakano-san?

—Of course you may.

—You may not know this, but Hiro once said that he knew how to help American soldiers get to Europe, I mean, you know, if they need to. Can you get me in touch with Hiro or tell him the next time you see him that I want to talk with him?

—I do know about these things. But Karen-san, you must never tell anyone at all. This is very dangerous because the Japanese government is a lackey of your government.

—A what?

—A lackey. It means "slave," I think. The Japanese are so afraid to do anything that will make Americans angry.

—You can trust me.

—Yes, I know. I can help you. I am the one who does this for Hiromasa and Emiko. I have an old school friend who is planning to help American soldiers get to the dock in Yokohama before they go to the Soviet Union and on to Europe. Is it Eric you are thinking about?

I paused and looked around the room.

—Yes. It's Eric.

—I see. We can get the soldiers out of Japan on a Soviet ship to Nakhodka. Then they take the train to Khabarovsk, and from there they go on an airplane to Moscow. Someone gets them from Moscow to Stockholm. I don't know about that.

—Thank you. Maybe it will be okay though. He is in Vietnam now, but he is coming back. Maybe they won't send him there for good.

—I hope not, Karen-san. I hope not.

The next day I got the letter, daddy. Until I opened it I had been feeling elated. Eric was coming back that weekend for one thing, and I was convinced that with Nakano-san's help we could save him from returning to Vietnam. But the letter destroyed me, daddy. It was from a woman named Fiona Willis.

20 December 1967

Dear Karen,

I am so so sorry to be writing this letter to you.

My name is Fiona Willis. I am British and I have been living here in Kathmandu with your brother Jeff pretty much since he arrived here in June '66.

Jeff died last night. I am so so sorry. We tried to do whatever we could to revive him and we eventually got him to the best hospital here. But he had taken an overdose of drugs and it was all too late.

Jeff was the kindest, tenderest and most compassionate person I have ever known. He never thought of himself. He always did things for people whenever they asked. He never cared a bit about money and he gave whatever he had to families here so that their children could go to school. Sometimes I had the devil's own job getting him to look after himself. He had a heart of gold. Karen, I am so so sorry.

A few days after he died a letter arrived for him from you, so that's how I knew how to write to you. I'm enclosing your letter together with this one. Jeff really didn't leave anything like possessions. He had said to me months ago that if anything happened to him, he wanted me to give his stuff to the Nepalese people. So, I have taken the liberty of doing that and I hope it is alright.

We didn't know what to do with Jeff's body, so we had it cremated. His ashes are kept at Boudhanath, the holy site here.

The monk said that he would keep Jeff's ashes safely if no one came to claim them.

I am going back to England to be with my family for Christmas and I don't think I will be coming back to Nepal. I must find a life for myself without Jeff now.

Jeff always told me so much about you, how sweet and kind you are and how close he was with you when you both were little. I wish I could meet you someday. I loved Jeff so much. I know I would love you too.

With an unending fondness,
Fiona

I felt numb all over. I couldn't focus my mind. I read the letter three times and still found myself not reacting. Maybe I didn't want to take it in then. It was as if Jeff's death was being blotted out of my mind, just like after that car accident I was in when I was thirteen and in a complete daze but didn't start shaking violently and crying my eyes out until that night. I knew the same thing was going to happen to me again. For a time I just sat in my room feeling totally empty.

The next day I wrote to you about Jeff's death. Remember? Maybe I should have phoned you, but I was afraid of what you might say to me. Who killed Jeff, daddy? Did he really kill himself?

Did reading my letter give you your first stroke in January? You recovered and wrote to me to say you were just fine and would be back to work in "a matter of weeks." You didn't even mention Jeff, daddy. Not a single word about Jeff! You've lost mom and Jeff, daddy. Everybody's abandoning you, everybody except me. That's why I've come back home. You still have me, daddy. I'm sitting with you here in the hospital right beside you. I'm still your little blueberry girl, as beautiful as ever.

I must have dozed off. The clock says 4:15. You are breathing regularly, and all of your tubes are where they should be. I'm completely numb all over. It's as if all feeling has been wiped from my skin. I still find it hard to believe that I will never see Jeff again. I knew that we would be so close to each other for the rest of our lives once we met again. Maybe it's really my fault, not yours, daddy. I could have gotten in touch with him earlier. If he had received my letter, he would have written back for sure. He would not have died without seeing me. But Nepal is so far from Japan, somehow much farther than America. Why didn't I write him earlier? Why didn't I ask him if he wanted to visit me? I was too bound up in myself, that's why. Maybe I could have saved him. You could have saved him, daddy. Did you write to him to tell him how much you disapproved of his "lifestyle"? Did you admonish him for not "doing something" with his life? He was doing something with his life, daddy. He was doing something wonderful and charitable and noble with his life.

What am I doing with my life? In a little over a month my life had tilted and shot off in a new direction. Is this what people call a tangent, as if you suddenly find yourself soaring through empty space off your normal orbit? Should I turn around, follow the line back and return to my "old" life, my "regular" life? Could I have turned back then even if I had wanted to? I could have gone back to living with the Rushes and returned to my classes on the base. Prof. Cromwell would have taken me under his wing. I would write an essay on the Japanese student movement. I would get credit for what I had "experienced" these past weeks. And in June I would have completed my course with flying colors, gone on home to L.A., spent summer reading pale paperbacks on the beach at Malibu and returned to U.S.C. for my sophomore year in September, telling my friends, such as they are, that, yeah, I'd been away and, yeah, I had a ball. Everything that happened to me in Japan would wash out of me and fade away, becoming a part of the watercolor past.

That's what you want for me, isn't it? "Keep it as a memory, Karen ... chalk it up to experience, put it under your belt and march forward to the future." Didn't you once say, "Everything in life is a phase"? What phase am I in now, daddy? A new moon is invisible. Is that what I am … a new moon?

The first days of January were a grim and uniform gray, perfect to suit my dismal mood. I was unused to the kind of cold that seeped in through the skin and spread slowly throughout the body. I felt as if nothing could warm me up. I thought of Eric constantly. He was coming back in a few days' time. But what if something happened to him, an accident in a jeep, a walk in the brush where there was a sniper waiting for an American, any American, to wander in? I had lost Jeff and I couldn't bear the thought of losing Eric too.

I asked Nakano-san if I could leave the store an hour early. It was the first Friday in January and only the second day after the new year that the store had been open.

—Not many people coming in yet. Please leave early.

—*Goshinsetsu ni arigato gozaimasu.* (That's very kind of you, thank you.)

—You should live forever in Japan, Karen-san. You will be just like us.

I put on two layers of sweaters below my brown duffel coat, wrapped my muffler around my neck and set out for Camp Zama. If I couldn't be with Eric, at least I could be close to where he lived. It was past six when I arrived at the base. It was already pitch dark. I stood by the fence where Eric had kissed me. About a dozen helicopters were parked on the airfield across the strip of lawn and, except for a couple of mechanics working on top of one of them, there was no one in sight. The big lights of the base were off. I put my fingers through the wire and spoke to myself.

—I'm here again, Eric. Right where you stood with me. I'm here and I can feel you. I know you're going to be all right. I know it.

Snow flurries were falling and I started to shiver. I crossed the street to The A Train. A sign on the door read "Yes, We Are Open." I put my hand on the doorknob but paused … a young woman all by herself in a place like that? I could hear Eric's voice clearly in my mind. "Not a good idea, baby, not a good idea."

But I had to go to the bathroom and was feeling very hungry. I turned the knob and entered. The same bald bartender with the goatee was behind the bar, polishing glasses. He looked up as I walked in, smiled, pointed a finger at me and nodded. There were only two people in the room, a middle-aged Negro couple sitting at the table where Eric and I had been. I walked up to the bar.

—*Obenjo ii desu ka*? (Toilet, all right?)

—Oh yes, please.

He pointed to a *noren* curtain hanging in a doorway in the corner behind the bar. When I came out of the bathroom there were two other people just sitting down at the table by the front door. My whole body shuddered. It was the two Americans who had come into the bookstore, the same ones who had written the note to me about Eric. I immediately turned toward the bar with my back to them.

—So, what would you like? Beer nuts again? How is Eric-san? I haven't seen him since you were here with him. Shall I play that song?

I was terrified. Why don't I just go up to them and greet them, feigning friendliness? They were probably absolutely harmless, just two young guys out for a good time. But their having asked about Eric in the note paralyzed me with fear, and I kept my back to them.

—Maybe you would like a soup instead? It is Campbell's Cream of Mushroom Soup, but I can make it hot for you. It is so cold in Tokyo now.

—Uh, no thank you.

The bartender stared at me. I didn't want to stay, and yet I was not able to budge from that spot at the bar. I would have to walk by their table to get to the door.

—I'm not hungry, thank you. I'm sorry. I'm sorry.

I could not stay there another minute. In any case, the two Americans were bound to come up to the bar to order. I wrapped my muffler over my head, covering my cheeks, and walked toward the door. They were looking intently at the menu together.

—Lookit, Chuckee, they've got "hambug" here. Shit on a stick, you'd think they'da learned plain English by now.

As I rushed past their table, the tall one, Chuck, raised his head from the menu.

—Hey, Frank.

Frank looked up.

—Hey, doll, where're you going so fast?

By then I had opened the door, shielding myself from them. I was certain that they hadn't recognize me. I was just another "doll" to them. The snow was now coming down heavily. I was shaking. I walked as quickly as I could in the direction of the station. I didn't turn around to look back for fear that the two of them would be standing in the doorway hoping to catch a glimpse of my face.

I came down with a cold the next day but continued to work in the store. Being the first weekend of the new year, Nakano-san put dozens of books on sale. We had a steady stream of customers coming in. It was startling to see how many Japanese people of all ages bought books in English. One customer, a young Japanese woman who looked like she was my age, asked for a book by Thomas Wolfe. I ran upstairs to my room where Eric had left "You Can't Go Home Again" and brought it down to her. She took it from me in both hands.

—Oh, this is just what I was looking for. Thank you so much. I am going to America to spend my junior year there.

I held the front door for her and watched her walk down the street. Was she going to go through the same sort of "phase" as me? She was so beautifully dressed in patent leather shoes, a navy blue skirt, white blouse, polka dot woollen vest with a beige and black striped jacket. Would she get to her city in America and fly off on a tangent, leaving the smooth circular path that, after a year, would have led her back to the same place again … home? I continued to watch her until she turned the corner at Iwanami Hall to descend the stairs into Jinbocho Station.

By Sunday afternoon I was feeling much better. I guess I had more of a chill than a cold. Nakano-san gave me an hour off so that I could rush over to Akihabara and buy an electric blanket.

—The sales are on now, and Akihabara is the best place to buy electric goods. Japanese people are finally able to afford the three c's.

—Three c's?

—Yes. Car, color television and cooler.

—Cooler? All I want is an electric blanket. It's freezing here.

—Yes, but in summer it is very *mushi-mushi*?

—*Mushi-mushi*? What's that?

—Just a moment please. Ah, my dictionary says "muggy."

—Oh, muggy. Well, you only learn words, I guess, when you go through experiences of them.

—You will be here in summer, too, Karen-san. I know. You will live with us.

I was back at the store a little after four with the box containing an electric blanket under my arm. There were two customers browsing. Nakano-san was behind the counter speaking with a middle-aged Japanese man in a dark brown felt hat. I put the box down and asked the customers if they would like some help. They nodded politely and continued to browse. Nakano-san shook hands with the man in the felt hat, who bowed his head as he brushed past me to leave.

—I'm back, Nakano-san. I'm sorry for abandoning you when you are so busy.

—Did you buy an electric blanket? Oh yes, I see you did.

—It was much cheaper there than the one's I've seen at the department stores in Shinjuku.

—Oh, you must never buy those things at a department store. They rip you up!

—What?

—They rip you up. It is a rip-up.

—You mean rip-off?

—Yes. I think so.

He chuckled, scratching his scalp.

That night I slept more soundly than I had since Eric left for Vietnam. He would be home soon and we weren't going to part again. That's what I believed, daddy. I truly believed it.

A few days later Eric phoned me in the evening. I almost tripped and fell as I ran down the stairs to get the phone.

—Hello, sweetheart. Hello?

—Baby, it's me.

—Oh God, I have missed you so much.

—Me too, me too. It was awful. I thought of you every minute.

—Me too.

—But I can't talk now, baby. I've got to hang up.

—But when can I see you?

—On the weekend. On Saturday. I'll come as early as I can and stay over. Is that what you want?

—Oh yes.

—I love you.

—I love you.

He hung up. I looked at the bookshelves against the far wall, where Eric's painting still hung. Despite their multicolored jackets, all the books seemed to merge into a solid gray shadow. Through the store window I could see cars driving by with their headlights on. It was raining heavily, and each time a car passed the store water splashed over the curb.

Eric had sounded so agitated. Something was wrong. Was he wounded or hurt in Vietnam? Did something horrible happen to him? Did he see something ghastly and terrifying? What was it that he couldn't tell me over the phone?

It was late Saturday afternoon when Eric walked into the bookstore. I was standing on a small ladder, shelving books. Nakano-san was in the storeroom. Eric came up to me from behind and grabbed my legs.

—Best legs in the Orient, bar none.

—Oh my God, you gave me a fright.

I looked around the store. We were alone. As I turned about on the ladder he lifted me down and kissed me on the lips.

—Eric, Nakano-san!

—He's not here, is he?

—I'm off in an hour, sweetheart.

—Can't wait an hour.

—You'll have to.

Nakano-san came out of the storeroom.

—Hello, Eric-san. Happy New Year.

—And a very happy New Year to you, too, Nakano-san. Thank you for looking after Karen.

—Oh, she looks after me, you know. She is like my daughter.

—Look, Eric, you go to a coffee shop or something and come back before six. Oh, and get something to eat, too, at the grocery store. Anything you like. Here's 1,000 yen. We'll eat in my room.

He left the bookstore, but stood on the sidewalk for a moment at the window, looking in. He smiled at me. He moved his lips to say "I love you" and turned swiftly away.

—I was so frightened that you were injured or something.

We were in my room lying on top of the futon after making love.

—I'm okay.

—Nobody, I mean, shot at you or ...

—No, baby, it's not like that. I didn't really go to the front line. Not where the VC are. That's next time.

—Next time?

—That's right. We were told in no uncertain terms that the fighting's going to get really bad in the spring and that's when we'll be sent back.

—You can't go.

—Can't go. Yeah. Tell me about it. One of the guys said he was going to eat half a bar of soap.

—What for?

—Gives you heart palpitations and they don't send you.

I sat up on my knees and took both his hands in mine.

—I had a word to Nakano-san. He can get you out of Japan to Europe.

—That's a big step, baby. One big step over half the world.

—Maybe. But dying ... I can't lose you. Are you hungry?

—I will be after I've had a bite out of you.

—But we just made love, Eric.

—So?

He smiled his big smile and put his hand on the small of my back, slowly lowering it. I knew then, daddy, that this was the man I was going to marry. I never thought for a minute that you'd approve. But do you approve of anything I do? Do you even know the woman your daughter has become? If you woke up now and looked at me would you recognize me? I sometimes think you wouldn't. "What are you doing in my daughter's birthday dress?" That's what you'd probably say. "Where's *my* blueberry girl?"

I'm here, daddy, beside you. I'm here for you.

Eric and I finished eating the rolled sushi he'd bought. He paced around the room.

—The trouble is, yeah, I wasn't injured, not in a physical way, but I can't just stand by and watch that stuff, baby. How can anyone watch that stuff? I'm just not strong enough inside.

—What stuff?

—The stuff that goes on there. It's worse than I had imagined. Worse than anyone could imagine. They're dropping napalm on those people in the villages. It's a kind of jelly that when it gets on you it burns the hell out of you right down to your bones, and your skin peels off and all you can do is run and run to get the wind to cool you off. I saw little kids, no bigger than five or six, getting it on them, all over their face and body, running around like wild animals and screaming for their mothers. But their mothers were either not there or dead on the ground.

—I thought you said you weren't on the front line.

—I wasn't. This was just a village out of Hue, the ones they call "hamlets," that our boys said they had pacified. Just an ordinary village full of rice farmers, most of them old people, women and children. The VC had long gone. That was obvious. But still, one of our guys shoved the butt of his rifle right in the face of an old man, like, for no reason at all. Smashed his whole face in. The old man sort of swung backwards and landed on his back. His head hit a rock and I think he was dead. A young woman, probably his daughter, put her baby down on a bench or something and ran to the old man. She cradled his head in her arms and wailed like, baby, like I've never heard wailing before. That wailing sound really got to me, went straight to my brain, baby. I can still hear it now.

Eric was standing beside me, squeezing my arm with force. I slipped it out of his grip.

—We left, I mean, me and the guys from Zama I went with, we left after that. But that night, I mean, one of the other guys from another unit who stayed in the village said that a few of the boys raped a young girl, maybe she was twelve or thirteen, maybe not even that, and then they set fire to her and the whole village with flame throwers they carry on their backs.

—Oh my God.

—That's right, baby. Oh my God! Oh my GOD! That's what we do. We're doing that.

Eric went to the window. He pushed open a curtain with the back of his hand and stared down at the street. I went to him and hugged him from behind.

—Sweetheart, I can't let you go back there. I'm not going to.

He pulled his hand off the curtain, turned toward me and put his arms around me, stroking my hair and kissing it.

—Yeah, I know, baby. Let's just see how things pan out. I may luck out. I may not have to go. They may keep me at Zama. Let's wait and see. Let's just wait and see.

—You can always come and live here. Nakano-san will protect you. He will make sure that no one finds out you are here.

—Yeah. But for how long? A week? A few weeks at most? How long could I hide out here if the MPs are after me, eh? You think they don't know things? I know those guys. They don't let people slip through their fingers like that. And the Japanese police do their bidding, so they got all angles cornered.

—Hiro or Emi could find a place for us.

—Hey, yeah, where are Hiro and Emi these days?

—I think they went to Kyushu or something. It's all been so hush-hush.

—Kyushu? What'd they go there for?

—I don't know.

—Oh yeah, the Enterprise.

He let go of me and laid down on my futon, resting a pillow on his stomach.

—Hey, what's this wire thingo?

—That's for my electric blanket.

—Oh, that's good. It keeps you warm when I'm not around.

—Eric.

—What?

—I went to Camp Zama when you were away.

—What? Why'd you do that, baby?

He tossed the pillow aside and sat up.

—Because I missed you, that's why.

—Baby, you can't do that! It's not a good idea. There are a million guys out there who are born on the other side of their prick, if you'll pardon my French. It's dangerous. They watch blue movies every night. They're all hepped up.

—But I went there to meet you before.

—And I was not in favor of that either, but at least I was with you. I don't want us seen together either.

—You don't?

—Hey, don't get all upset. Stop crying, baby. I didn't mean it that way. I mean, I don't want us seen together where anyone in the military might see us.

—I'm sorry. I just ...

He stood up, grabbed my hands and pulled me down onto the futon. He started kissing my face and hair and neck. Then he unbuttoned my dress, took off my bra and undies and kissed me everywhere. I'll stop there, daddy. I don't think you want to hear the "gory details," as you used to call them, not at least when they're details connected to your own daughter. Besides, it's twenty minutes to five and I've got other things to tell you before the doctor comes at six. So breathe regularly, daddy, and listen to me.

Two weeks passed. I worked every day, staying in my room in the evenings to study Japanese and saving up as much money as I could. If Eric did go into hiding, I wanted to be able to support him until he got safely away. I borrowed a tape recorder from Nakano-san and bought Japanese language tapes that I kept on all the time, even when I was asleep. Every night at 7:30 on the button Eric phoned. But we didn't talk about anything important. Eric told me when he was in my room that the phones on the base are probably bugged. So, on the phone I only talk about things like the bookstore, new Japanese words I've learned and whatever I know about the Rushes.

Dr. Ben called me when they came back from Okinawa. He said that Jeanette and Fran had a great time. They loved being on the beach there, which is "kind of a scaled-down Santa Monica without the pier," and you can get anything you want like Coke and candy bars like Abba-Zaba and American cigarettes just as cheap as at the PX. He said the girls had plenty of American boys to flirt with there, even Fran, who's started wearing makeup, "but only when we let her go out."

Dr. Ben had heard from you, daddy.

—Your father's stroke was very minor and he's apparently fully recovered and back driving his fabulous Buick convertible around L.A.

—I wrote him a letter but he didn't answer.

—Well, I think he's worried because you left the base.

—Angry would be more like it. He's shutting me out.

—He wouldn't do that. He does love you, Karen. That's why he isn't writing. Can you understand that?

—Not really.

When I told Eric over the phone about the conversation I had with Dr. Ben, he seemed alarmed.

—You haven't told the Rushes about me, have you?

—No, of course not. What do you take me for? But I did say to one of the girls that I had a boyfriend. But that's all.

—But do they really know?

—What, that we're boyfriend and girlfriend? Yes, I just said so.

—No. That I'm not white.

I paused, holding the receiver against my cheek.

—I thought so.

—I just couldn't blurt it out, Eric, could I?

—Blurt it out?

—I mean, you know, I couldn't just tell her. You think I'm ashamed or something? Or afraid? I'm the one who wants to go to your base and be together all the time everywhere. When I get you home I'm going to put on my best bikini and parade your big black body all the way from Malibu to Venice Beach.

—Is that a long way?

—It's half a world in L.A. Nothing else much counts where I come from.

On Saturday night the 3rd of February Hiro and Emi came to my room above the bookstore. Eric had been there all day waiting for me to finish work. I had bought all the ingredients I needed to make sukiyaki, and Nakano-san had loaned me an electric frying pan that you just plugged in to heat up. Hiro brought the hugest bottle of sake I've ever seen. We hadn't been with the two of them since they went to Kyushu.

—Emi and I came back to Tokyo last week, but we have been so busy with student meetings.

—What happened in Kyushu, Hiro?

—I think Emi should tell, Eric. Her English is much better.

—Emi?

—We all met at Fukuoka. Students came from all over Japan, but some were arrested before they got to Kyushu. Police were looking for students at stations in Tokyo and Osaka who carried *gevabo* or wore helmets. At first I stayed at the dormitory in Kyushu University. We collected big rocks and made broken bricks to throw at the riot police, because we knew they would attack us. On January 18th the USS Enterprise came into Sasebo. The huge aircraft carrier, like a world unto itself, sailed into this tiny little Japanese port. It was like a floating Gulliver. But we little people are many. So many student groups were there. We don't like each other. In Europe students fight the police. In Japan students fight each other. But in Kyushu we stopped fighting, because we have a common enemy.

—Were the riot police there already, I mean, when you got there?

—Oh yes. Maybe five thousand. I went to Hirase Bridge, that's where the naval base is, after a couple of days. The roads were blocked with armored cars, and the police were waiting for us like starving cats sitting perfectly still for their plump little mice to come along. They hid behind barricades with barbed wire on top. They had these big hoses on trucks to spray us, and they had tear gas too. We did a snake dance chanting peace slogans, and thousands of ordinary people watched and chanted with us, many old people and women too. But the *uyoku* were there too. They are the fascists who stand with the police. The police then rushed into the open and came at us with shields. They struck us everywhere, over and over again. We had helmets on and cloths over our mouths and thick white *guntei* gloves on, but they struck us with their big sticks on our backs and behind our knees first. I escaped, but many students were hurt badly and arrested, and many riot policemen were injured too. I went back to the dormitory in Fukuoka, but the riot police were there too. At night they put on big searchlights and they ran in, bashing us when we were asleep. Many students had to be taken to the hospital. Some of them must have got brain damage.

—You're lucky to get back here in one piece.

—Maybe. But this is not the end, Eric. The Enterprise has nuclear power and maybe even nuclear bombs on it. The Japanese government will not say, because it is illegal to bring nuclear weapons into Japan. So they just shut their mouth like a marionette with the string pulled up. Sasebo is only fifty kilometers from Nagasaki, and people remember the atom bomb that was dropped there twenty-three years ago. But the Japanese government wants Japanese people to like nuclear power, so they can someday build a bomb. This is the worst thing. So Japan gives money and everything to America for Vietnam. We saw many American soldiers with Japanese girls at night in Sasebo. Just like after the war. Japan is America's happy little prostitute. We love to be fucked.

Emi looked straight at me when she said that, but I wasn't going to act like the shy girl I was when I first met her.

—Hey, anyone want more sukiyaki?

Hiro filled Eric's empty tumbler with sake, then topped up mine. I lifted it up to make a toast.

—I propose a toast. To the greatest year yet, 1968. Robert Kennedy will be the next president and he will get us out of Vietnam. Then we won't have to be suspicious of each other. And when we fuck, Emi, it will be because both of us want to. Oh, pardon my French.

Emi cocked her head back and raised her eyebrows. Eric downed his tumbler and held it up in front of Hiro.

—I'll have another drink. This one is to Robert Kennedy. I just hope he gets in before every last American boy has to go to Vietnam.

We all clinked glasses. Then, suddenly, a shadow passed over Eric's face.

—The Viet Cong started a new attack a couple of days ago. It may turn into a huge offensive for them. They even managed to hit Saigon. It looks like spring is coming a little early this year to Vietnam.

—Don't say that, Eric.

—It's true whether I say it or not.

Emi turned on me.

—So what have *you* done to stop all this? It's your country committing these crimes.

—You can't ... why are you saying this, Emi? What have I done to you? Eric's American too. And you even said that Japanese are complicit. Does that make you guilty too?

—Eric can't help it. He was drafted. You didn't have to come here and live on a base. You did it of your own volition.

—I left, didn't I? I left the base. I quit the university because what I was learning was useless crap. What else do you want me to do, get a bomb and blow up the American embassy?

I stood up, went to my little kitchen area and started to wash the dishes.

—Hey, baby, don't be like that. Emi was just ...

—I'm fine, Eric. Somebody's got to do the dishes.

The three of them sat there drinking sake and talking about the war. You remember the war, daddy, don't you? You said, "We'll go in and mop the place up of commies and be out by Christmas." Which Christmas were you talking about then, daddy? It's still going strong. You even tried to convince Jeff to sign up and said you could use some pull to get him into officer training. Jeff said he would take a knife and cut the skin between his thumbs and index fingers so he wouldn't be able to pull a trigger. He even got out his old switchblade with the ivory handle, the one you gave him for his tenth birthday. But he ended up going to Nepal instead, disappearing so the draft board couldn't find him. He disappeared, daddy. He fell off your radar. And then he went up and died on you, daddy. You would have been proud of him if he had died in Vietnam, so you should be just as proud of him now. He made a life for himself. For *himself*, daddy. There was no other life he could have had. He certainly didn't want yours or anything like it. The war sent him away just as it was about to send Eric away. I wasn't going to let what happened to Jeff happen to Eric, though. I wasn't going to let Eric be the casualty of the war your son became.

In the late afternoon of that Sunday the two soldiers from Camp Zama showed up at the bookstore. Eric was upstairs reading, and Nakano-san was in the storeroom unloading a new shipment of books that had arrived from England the day before. The shorter soldier, who was very muscular, did most of the talking.

—Howdy. Remember us, the two lonesome cowpokes?

I decided that a bright friendliness was my best defence.

—Sure I do. You were looking for a book about Japanese planes. Find something?

—See, Chuck, I told you she'd remember us. You know, we were rather, uh, you know, blunt, I mean, forward the last time we were here. I want to sincerely apologize to you.

—Oh, no need to apologize at all.

—Very kind of you to say so. We were sort of blunt because we didn't even introduce ourselves. I'm Frank, Frank Houseman, and this here is Chuck McTern. Chuck's from Plattsmouth, Nebraska and I'm from Oxford. That's Oxford, Mississippi, but I tell everybody I went to school at Oxford. Can put on a pretty convincing Oxford accent too, so lots of people can't really tell at first.

—Nice to meet you.

—Can we ask your name, please?

—Sure. Uh, it's Jeanette.

—Nice to meet you, Jeanette.

They both put out their hands at the same time, and I didn't know which to shake first.

—One at a time, Chuck. Steady, boy.

Frank slapped Chuck on the back of his hand.

—Chuck and me thought y'all might reconsider, you know, just showing us the lights and things.

—Thank you very much, but I rarely go out at night.

—Hey, this could be the exception that proves the rule.

—It's very kind of you, but I, uh, I ...

I was hoping that Nakano-san would come in so I could hand the two of them over to him.

—So, Jeanette, who's this Eric dude anyways?

Chuck was looking around the room. From where he was standing he could see the stairs going up to my room between bookshelves. Should I have just walked away there and then? They might have taken that as an insult and become even more pushy.

—I don't see him anymore.

—Why, that's great, then, that's just great. So there's nothin' stoppin' you.

—Look, I'm very busy here at the store every day, including Saturdays and Sundays. And at night I don't go out, I just study.

—All work and no play, is it? You know, we thought that just by coincidence this Eric guy, now, heck, I suppose you're not seein' him no more, but by chance he might be where we are, you know, at Camp Zama. So we did some snoopin', and there are three Erics on the base, but two of them are married and the other one's a, well, a Negro. So we figured he must be someone else.

—He's not in the army, I mean, he wasn't in the army. I'm not going out with him anymore.

—Oh, one of those *gaijin* guys who comes here and surrounds himself with little Jap cutie-pies, some professor or something, is he? We can't compete with a dude like that.

—Speak for yourself, Frank.

—Y'all will have to forgive Chuck here. He fancies himself a ladies' man. No, we couldn't believe it was the other Eric out at Zama, not a nice girl like you with a … with a colored. I mean, I swear, one of them saved my life out of Danang last year, and I ain't got nothin' against 'em so long as they keep their hands where they belong.

—Yeah, in their own pants.

—Now, Chuck, don't be crude in front of the lady. Didn't ya hear? They're havin' a Negro astronaut. They're gonna send him in space and let the whole world know that the jig is up.

Chuck hit Frank's bicep with his fist, and they burst into laughter. Frank laughed so hard that he started to cough.

—Look, thanks a lot but I've got work to do.

—Oh, we came in so you could work. For us. I mean, we still want that book, an' you're the one who can get it for us, right?

—Which book?

Chuck was now looking at the books behind him. I turned around and caught sight of Eric standing on one of the bottom stairs of the staircase. If they saw him they would put two and two together. I couldn't let that happen.

—Hey, we've got those books over here, the ones you wanted.

—I took Frank by the elbow and led him to the middle section of one of the bookshelves. Chuck, however, stayed where he was. He took a big picture book down from one of the upper shelves and started leafing through it.

—Hey, Jeanette, that's more like it. We're promenading here together. Do-si-do and all the way home.

Luckily Nakano-san had just appeared behind the counter,

carrying a stack of books up to his chin. I threw him a glance to indicate that I needed his help. He dropped the books on the counter and came up to us.

—Can I help you gentlemen? Oh, you were looking for books on Japanese aircraft, am I not correct? I have something very rare for you. You must see it.

I pulled my hand out from between Frank's elbow and side.

—Well, gentlemen, I'll leave you in Mr. Nakano's capable hands.

—Come this way into the storeroom. What I want to show you is so valuable that I keep it there. It is a copy of Life magazine from November 1942 with an article about the Zero. That is what you wanted, is it not? Best fighting plane in the world at the time, as I am sure you know. You can be proud, too, because the engine was copied from your country's engine by Pratt & Whitney.

Nakano-san made sure that they were in front of him as he directed them into the storeroom. I rushed to the bottom of the stairs. Eric was standing on the second stair.

—Eric, you've got to go back up now.

—Why, baby?

—It's those two creepy guys from the base. They know your name.

—What? How do they know me?

—I don't know. They looked it up or something. They can't know that you're here.

—They're not going to find that out. I just want to get some fresh air. Been cooped up all day.

I heard Nakano-san clearing his throat as he stepped out of the storeroom.

—That's funny. I was sure the magazine was in the storeroom.

I gave Eric a push on his thigh.

—Just go back up now. Please.

He peered into the bookstore, exchanged glances with Nakano-san, turned around and bounded up the stairs. I looked toward Nakano-san. Frank, who was standing beside him, waved to me. I smiled, followed Eric up the stairs, went into my room and locked the door behind me.

—So who were those guys anyway?

—I have no idea. They've been coming in and writing me notes. They give me the creeps.

—Writing you notes? What kind of notes?

—I don't know, Eric. It's nothing serious. They're just out on a lark or something.

—Out on a lark, yeah. I know what those larks are like. I've seen dudes like them. You stay away from them. That's what I meant about you going near the base.

—I will stay away from them. I don't want them to find out about you. That's what I'm worried about.

—How could they? I've never seen them in my life.

Eric put his arms around me and kissed me.

—I've got to get back to work.

—Just a few minutes. Take a break.

—Not now, sweetheart. I've really got to get back.

—Okay, me too. I've got to get back to my reading. I'm learning for the first time what it means to be black. Funny that I had to come all the way to Japan to find that out.

On the table there were six or seven books by Richard Wright, James Baldwin, Ralph Ellison and LeRoi Jones.

—Me too. I had to come to Japan to find out what it means to be white.

He grabbed me and started to kiss me again.

—Not now, Eric. I said not now!

I smiled at him and blew him a kiss from the doorway. I walked down the stairs very slowly, bending forward to look into the store when I was halfway down. Nakano-san was behind the counter with a pencil in his hand, writing the price on the title page of books. I could only see a small part of the store, but it appeared as if the two soldiers had left. I continued down the stairs. Nakano-san looked up and nodded. The Americans had gone.

That night Nakano-san came upstairs after closing the store and knocked on my door.

—It is Nakano. May I come in?

—Yes, of course.

I opened the door and let him in. Eric stood up from the table and shook hands with him.

—Mr. Nakano, I cannot thank you enough for all that you are doing for Karen, and for me.

—It is the least I can do for you. May I sit down?

—*Dozo okake kudasai.* (Please have a seat.)

—Oh, Karen-san, I am more and more amazed at your politeness.

—Karen, make him a cup of coffee or something.

—Oh no, I am fine, thank you.

The three of us sat down and, for a moment, no one spoke.

—Eric-san, how are you?

—I'm fine, thank you. And thanks to Karen, who looks after me.

—It is nice to have someone to look after you. My wife died last year.

—Oh, I'm sorry to hear that, Mr. Nakano.

—How terrible for you.

—Thank you both. We had no children, but Hiromasa is like my child. And now so are you, Karen-san.

—You are my Japanese father.

—Thank you. I want to be called that. That's why I said Hiromasa was like my son. So that you would say that.

We all laughed. Eric leaned forward.

—Do you live nearby, I mean, in the vicinity of ...?

—Yes I do. I have a very small apartment at Hanzomon, but my parents' home is in Nakarokugo. It's a working class part of Tokyo where there are little factories. It was badly destroyed by fire from American bombs, but it is now back to the way it was. Because I did not go to war, I stayed with my mother when my father took a job with Mantetsu, the Manchurian Railway Company run by the Japanese. He went there alone. Six years after the end of the war, my father came back from the Soviet Union where he was a prisoner in camps. He was captured in Manchuria in August 1945. When the Red Army came into Manchuria, the Kantogun, that's the Japanese army in Manchuria, ran away south to save themselves and left all the civilians working there, like my father, to be captured. The camps in Siberia were very hard, but my father was a communist before the war so he was happy to be in the Soviet Union. He did not come back to Japan until 1951. Their little house in Nakarokugo was used by them as a meeting place for working people. So, people there don't like the police. They had bad feelings about the police from the wartime. Here is a map of Nakarokugo. It is near Kamata Station. The house is empty now.

—Kamata? Isn't that where the protests against Sato's visit to Vietnam and the U.S. took place, where students were beaten by the riot police last year?

—Yes, Eric-san, it is. But that was closer to the airport. I am far from that place. This is my house here, where I have made an X. No one has lived in it for a year. I moved out last year when Shizue died, to be closer to my bookstore. This is the telephone number there. I wrote it at the bottom of the map.

—Why are you showing us this, Nakano-san?

—Because, Karen-san, you never know when you might have

to move out of here.

—Why would I move out? I'm not going back to Tachikawa, if that's what you mean.

—Not to Tachikawa. But at some time it may become dangerous for you and Eric-san to live here. The Japanese police came here. They may want to arrest Hiromasa and Emiko. There will be many more bloody demonstrations. If you wish to, you can move to my home in Nakarokugo and live there as long as you like. The only other people who know about the house are Hiromasa and Emiko. No one in Nakarokugo bothers about whether someone is a *gaijin* or not. Across the street and up the road from my house is a Lutheran church. Here, I will make another X. The pastor is Dr. Roggen. He is German. He has lived in Japan for more than fifty years, even during the war. He is a pacifist and he will help you if you need something. Oh, and here is the key. I am sorry but I have only one key.

Nakano-san put the key on top of the map, stood, bowed, said *ojama shimashita* and left.

—What's that he said?

—It means "I'm sorry to have disturbed you."

—I never thought you might have to move out. It's because of me, isn't it.

—No, it isn't! It's not because of you. Not everything is because of you, you know.

—Yeah, that's right. I know. I'm an invisible man.

—Eric, stop feeling sorry for yourself. It's because of me. He's afraid the police will find me. I'm not supposed to be living or working here. My address and status are written on my alien registration card. They say I live in Tachikawa and am a student. Now, come here, invisible man. You read too much, that's your problem.

The next day, Monday, was a holiday. The day commemorating

the foundation of the Japanese nation in 660 B.C. fell on the Sunday, so the holiday was celebrated on Monday. I couldn't believe how they knew that the nation was founded on the 11th of February in 660 B.C. Nakano-san closed the store, but not because it was a holiday. He said, "This is a new holiday in Japan. We Japanese have so few real holidays, we have to make up new ones." It was the first anniversary of his wife's death and he didn't want to work. Eric was back at Camp Zama, so I decided to do some exploring and see where Nakano-san's house was. I had never been to that part of Tokyo. But I misread the train line map and got off two stops before Kamata at Ikegami. According to Nakano-san's map there was an old temple called Honmonji not far from Ikegami Station. When I arrived there at about 11:00 the air was so bright that my eyes hurt when I looked at the sky. A warm breeze was blowing. Could spring already have come, or was this just the false promise of a new season? The long stone sweep of steps leading up to the temple came into sight. Men in slacks and jackets were leading neatly dressed little children by the hand up the steps, followed by women in colorful kimonos, laboriously lifting their feet in order to climb. A sign in English at the bottom of the steps said that its stones were laid in 1603. When I reached the top of the steps I could see a path turn off to the right where a pagoda towered over hundreds of old graves. In the square in front of the temple people were standing beside an enormous bronze pot filled with ash and incense sticks, waving their hands like fans to get as much incense smoke as they could over their faces. I walked among the graves. Some people were pouring water over the gravestones or putting little bottles of sake, tangerines and plastic flowers below them.

Behind the temple I found myself in a huge garden of plum blossom trees. The trees were decked in a full bloom of red, white and pink flowers. I sat on a bench, looked up to the sky and shut my eyes. The warmth of the sun seemed to wash over my entire body. I didn't feel cold at all. I listened closely to the sounds around me … children shrieking in the distance, birds chirping, the lingering gong of a temple bell. Maybe I'm getting used to it. Maybe I belong here and not in America. I kept my eyes shut for a long time and, when I opened them, the sky had clouded over and turned flat gray.

A little boy ran up to me.

—*Obasan, Amerikajin?* (Are you an American?)

I smiled, stood and walked past him without answering. But I could hear his voice coming from behind.

—*Amerikajin, Amerikajin, Amerikajin da!* (She's an American, an American, an American!)

I took the train to Kamata, where I ate lunch at a restaurant specializing in sardine dishes, and walked for about fifteen minutes until I found Nakano-san's house. It was more a shack than a house, wedged between run-down apartment blocks. So this was where Nakano-san lived. Would I ever end up living there? If I did, daddy, it would be a world away from Pacific Palisades, I can tell you that. There was no driveway there for one thing. Mom used to say, "You can always judge a house by its driveway." But I knew I could live there. I didn't care for how long. I was already more than a world removed from all that I was before.

It's ten minutes to five, daddy, and I don't feel sleepy anymore. I am staring at your face and wondering if what I've been telling you has been getting through to you. Maybe it's been all too distant. After all, Japan, plum blossoms, sardine restaurants, books written by Negroes, students wearing helmets and wielding big sticks … it's all unrelated to you, isn't it. I can hear you say, "Come back down to earth, Karen. Live where you belong! Be with your own." Okay, let's get closer to home. Let's get down to the nitty-gritty. If anything will get a rise out of you it will be this. I mean, all this talk of me and my boyfriend and Japanese people you have no conception of … I don't blame you for just lying there as if you were nearly dead. It's time I told you something about yourself. Oh, you know this better than anybody, daddy. You know every gory detail. All I know is what I heard from Myra and Mieko. This happened to you, daddy. This is your life, Dr. George Rogers.

The thing they both mentioned right at the beginning was the venetian blinds. When you had them alone in the house, you went from room to room closing the blinds. Myra told me that she even asked you why you were doing it and you said, "I like my privacy." Ring a bell? You remember that, don't you, daddy? You like your privacy, don't you? Whatever you've done in life that you might regret, you've cherished your privacy. "Keep it under your hat, will you? Don't you ever say that again! Don't you breathe a word of it, do you hear? You don't know what you're talking about!" Well, daddy, I know. I KNOW! And I want you to know that. I want you to hear what my friends told me about you. This should be the test. If you don't react to this, then maybe you won't ever react to anything again.

You tried to rape them, daddy. Your M.O. was the same. Sorry to be sounding like Jack Webb, but that's the only language you understand. Just the facts. You went from room to room, closing the blinds. Then you went up to Mieko, who was only fifteen, daddy, fifteen! It was October and it was her first time in the U.S., and she was terrified. She told me that after it was over she went into the bathroom and threw up. You were nearly twice as big as her and you stood in front of her and loosened your belt. She tried to walk away from you, but you grabbed her arm from behind and said, "Don't be afraid." You led her into the master bedroom. That's a good one. Master bedroom! She told me that she was shaking all over. You began to unbutton her blouse and she kept saying "No no no" over and over again. You took hold of her skirt and pulled it down to her ankles. She said that she was going to scream. You said that no one would hear her, that you lived in a very big house with a very long driveway. You took off your trousers and underwear and put her hand on your penis, daddy. Mieko said to me that she had never been with a man before. Are you proud of that, daddy? You were to be her first. She started to weep, daddy. Even in wartime some men soften when they see a woman weeping. Did you soften, daddy? Did your heart go out to her? Did you think even for an instant that you were about to scar this young girl for life in your chamber bedroom, in your master bedroom? Oh, I see that this is having an effect. You are beginning to breathe heavily. This heavy breathing is causing your head to bob. Are you recalling the little girl's soft hand on your swollen penis, daddy, on your penis all pumped up with your blood, is that what you're thinking about, is that what's causing your head to bob … or are you nodding to me, saying to me, "Okay okay you know, yes, I hear you, Karen, I hear you loud and clear, I know what you are saying, but what gives you the right to talk to your father like this, how can you even dare to mention such things to him, you are my child and you have no idea what you're talking about, shut up, Karen, just shut your goddamn trap! I will not listen to this anymore! Go away! Leave this room forever! Let me die in peace" … is that what you're dying to tell me, daddy?

But Myra wouldn't go along with it, would she, daddy? She was eighteen and not a demure little Japanese girl like Mieko. "Dr. Rogers, why are you shutting the venetian blinds?" she asked, and you said, "I like my privacy." She realized then what you were planning to do to her, and she ran for the front door. But you got there before she could unhook the chain. You pushed her to the side and pressed yourself against her. Her back was to the wall, daddy. You like that, people with backs against the wall? All she could do was surrender. You could have your way with her, couldn't you. You removed your belt and held it in front of her face like a weapon. She told me everything, daddy, everything! She squirmed her way out and ran to the bathroom, but you caught her before she could get in and lock the door, and you pulled her back into the living room and you threw her against an armchair. You lifted up her skirt and pulled her underwear off, but she wouldn't stop kicking, would she, daddy? How did it feel to see her fighting back like that? Did that raise your hackles, daddy, did it fire you up? You tried to hold her hands still but she was too strong. She shoved you away and screamed at the top of her lungs. "Help!" she screamed. "Someone, help!" Did you suddenly feel sorry for her, daddy? You should have. But instead you said something else, didn't you? You said, "You disgust me!" That's what you said, daddy. Amazing. No, not amazing ... "heavy." That's what your son Jeff would have said. He wasn't dead then, daddy. It's a shame he never found out about you. It's a real shame I never had the chance to tell him about his holier-than-thou exceptional father!

Myra remembered it all down to the last detail. She disgusted you, did she? Why? Because she wouldn't give in to you? Because at that very moment she became a threat to you? Come on, what are you worried about? No one would believe a young girl's story about an eminent chest specialist, ex-president of the California Thoracic Association. Ah, maybe it occurred to you then that she might tell me. Your own daughter would find out about you, find out that her father is a rapist. So you stopped there, didn't you, daddy? You held yourself back. You controlled yourself. You kicked Myra's undies to her and said, "Don't you dare ever breathe a word of this to anyone." And you repeated to her what you said to her before. "You disgust me." That's heavy, daddy-o, heavy. Myra dressed and ran out of the house. She said that she didn't know where to go. She ran and ran until she got to a gas station and locked herself in the bathroom there. I came back home from the hospital with mom and Myra wasn't there. I remember asking you where she was, and you said you didn't know, that she went out to the movies or somewhere. She came back just as it was getting dark and went to her room without eating dinner. After dinner I went to her room and asked if anything was the matter, and she said she was fine and that was all. She didn't tell me about what you did to her until a year later, when I met her for lunch at the U.S.C. cafeteria. But you knew, daddy, that I would never bring it up with you, didn't you? That was your protection ... my silence. Well, I've broken that silence now, and I can see that you are responding to me. Bravo, daddy, bravo! You're gasping for breath now. Should I press the button and buzz for the little green intern? Maybe he'd come in and try the same thing on me. Oh, you wouldn't like that, would you? You wouldn't allow that, would you? You'd sit up in bed and give him a good talking-to, throw the book at him, would you? No, I can't risk calling him. We'll just have to wait it out. Now you're not breathing at all. Ten seconds ... eleven ... twelve ... twenty ... twenty-one ... oh, that's a long time between breaths, daddy, you'd better start breathing again. Oh, your legs just stiffened. Is that because you're not breathing? Am I being cruel? What do you want me to do? Should I call in Chuck? It may be all in my imagination that he would come at me again. We women exaggerate these things, don't we? Aw, come on, it was nothing, forget it. After all, what's more important, my little anxieties or your life? I'm looking at the clock, daddy. It's already five. Don't make me use the button. Just pull through this one and you've got only another hour to wait before Dr. Cohen arrives. He'll know what to do. He'll be able to deal with this. So I'll just sit back in my chair and hope that you can work this one out by yourself, daddy. I'm leaving you to your own devices. If my telling your story back to you ends up upsetting you, I am genuinely sorry. But it's nothing that you didn't know already. It's nothing new under the sun, is it?

The news coming out of Vietnam was bleak. The Viet Cong offensive had reached Saigon. I now had a transistor radio that I listened to at night, bedded up in my futon. My Japanese was at the stage where I could get the gist of most news reports. Student unrest was growing in Europe and the U.S., and people were predicting mass demonstrations in Japan too.

One day toward the end of February Hiro and Emi showed up at the bookstore in the late afternoon. Nakano-san let them in, put the "CLOSED" sign in the window and pulled the shade down over the door.

—But it isn't closing time, Nakano-san.

—I know. We are closing early today.

Emi lifted herself up to sit on the counter.

—*She* doesn't have to stay here. I don't want to talk with her here.

The way she emphasized *she* cut me to the bone.

—No, she can stay, Emiko-san. Let her stay. She may need to know.

There was a knock at the shop door. Nakano-san pulled the side of the shade toward him and peeked out, then opened the door just enough for a man to come in. It was the man in the brown felt hat who had been in the store some weeks earlier.

—This is Iwabuchi-san.

He took off his hat and bowed to us.

—Iwabuchi-san, this is Karen-san. She works for me.

—How do you do? I am Shozo Iwabuchi.

—*Hajimemashite. Karen Rojazu to moshimasu.* (Nice to meet you. My name is Karen Rogers.)

—She is learning Japanese very quickly.

—Oh, Nakano-san, you are much too kind.

—You see? She has even mastered our false modesty.

Everyone chuckled at this except Emi. Iwabuchi-san told us how he managed to get another American *dassohei* out of Japan. I didn't know the word but I could guess what it meant … "deserter."

—We arranged for a few of our Soviet friends to meet him at a coffee shop in Yokohama, where they passed him a Soviet passport. When it got dark and a ship, the Ordzonikidze, was about to leave port, they pretended they were drunk and staggered arm in arm to the dock. The Russians spoke Russian and waved their passports in front of the Japanese customs officials' faces. The officials laughed and waved the three of them on. The Ordzonikidze departed for Nakhodka and that was it. Last year we managed to get four sailors from the Intrepid to Moscow too, though that was much more tricky.

Emi took Iwabuchi-san's hat from his hands and put it on the counter.

—You are saving not only the life of one American, you are saving the lives of the many Vietnamese men, women and children he would have killed.

Hiro pointed a finger in the air.

—Wait a minute, Emi, you can't say that for sure. The thing is that, I mean, it is the one American whose life is just as …

—Hiro, you have no idea, do you? He would have gone to Vietnam for sure. Do you know what they're doing over there?

—Yes, but this one American may not have done those things. It's enough to save one life, isn't it? It's a matter of conscience.

—Conscience? Give me a break. What kind of conscience do

people have who murder babies in front of their mothers and ...

—Stop arguing, you two. Hiromasa, go and make some tea for our guests.

—Yes, Uncle.

Hiro went into the storeroom to make tea.

—Karen-san.

—Yes.

—Iwabuchi-san can help Eric, if it becomes necessary.

—Oh, I don't think Eric wants that. He wants to be able to return to America and live there. His father is there.

—Yes, I understand.

Some moments later Hiro came back, carrying a tray with a small cream-colored teapot and five cups. He carefully poured green tea for us.

—I'll go back and refill the pot with hot water.

—No. It's more important that you stay here, Hiro.

—No, Emi, actually, I'm going. I'm leaving. I'm sorry, Uncle, but I don't think I should be a part of this. Goodbye, Karen. Please say hello to Eric-san from me.

—Sure, Hiro.

—Thank you. Bye bye.

Hiro left. As I went up to my room, the two Japanese men were standing by the counter. Emi, sitting on it, was speaking to them and gesticulating unlike any Japanese woman I have seen, as if giving a speech to a crowd of people. I stood at my window for some time before I saw Iwabuchi-san leave the store, followed by Emi and Nakano-san. It would be over an hour before Eric phoned. I wanted him so much to phone right then. I wanted to tell him what happened in the store, but I knew it was unwise to do it over the phone. I wanted him to tell me that he was fine, that he had been given new duties at the base that would tie him down there, that he would never be ordered to Vietnam and not have to make a choice that might part us for God knows how long. But these things were out of my hands. They were out of his hands too. In whose hands were they? Who decided these things, whether a man would be sent to another country to kill people? Is it you, daddy … or like Emi said, is it me, after all?

That Saturday night Eric was more distraught than I had ever seen him. Even when we made love he seemed distracted. I asked him what was troubling him.

—Nothing. It's nothing. Just the whole thing. It's gotten under my skin.

—What whole thing?

—I'm kind of wedged in, stuck, I mean, pinned down. I can't move. I can't go forward and I can't go back. I'm being slowly crushed to death by the suit of armor put around me by my country. It's too small for me and it's crushing me to death, Karen.

—Sorry, I don't get it. What's happening?

—They're moving guys out of Japan because of the Tet offensive. You heard about that, didn't you, on your Japanese transistor. My number is going to come up sooner or later. I at least thought I'd be able to hold on till the summer and then, I don't know, I thought that the presidential campaign would kind of make people think twice about going in strong in Vietnam. Johnson's bombing the fucking hell out of the north. Sorry, baby, sorry for swearing.

—It's all right, sweetheart. I can see how upset you are.

—I can't take it, baby. I can't take it any longer!

Tears welled in his eyes. I hugged him tightly.

—Shh. We're going to be all right.

—I keep hearing the wailing of that woman in the village. I keep seeing little naked kids with their skin hanging off them like tissue paper, running in all directions, wailing at the top of their lungs. I see fire, baby, fire racing through the air and landing on the straw roof of a hut. People run out. They're coughing their guts out. They fall on the ground. American soldiers kick their heads in, baby. They drag the women away into the brush, three or four men on one woman. I can hear them laughing. Then, finally …

—Shh. I'm here with you. Shh.

—No, I want to say this … then, finally, when they're all over with her, one guy takes his gun out and shoots the woman, who's lying on the ground, in the back of the head. Baby, I can't watch that again. I can't go to a place where I have to see that. I don't care what happens to me … but I can't go.

I held his head against my chest and stroked his face. Nakano-san was right. I did need to know what the man in the brown felt hat could do for us.

Everything changed on Wednesday the 6th of March. It was early afternoon, the time of day when we saw few customers. Nakano-san had gone out. I was tending the store by myself. The front door opened with a ring of the little bell above it and the American soldier named Frank walked in alone.

—Howdy. All alone, are we?

—Yes. May I help you?

—Yes you may, *Karen*.

He looked around the room, humming a tune below his breath.

—I don't give out my name to strangers.

—Well, I didn't think we were exactly strangers. You know, we have met several times now, even once out at Camp Zama, or should I say not far from Camp Zama, at a little place called The A Train. Oh yes, I noticed you. Y'all can't hide your little old self under a scarf. But you seemed to be in a hurry, so I just let sleeping dogs lie.

—Mr. Nakano should be back any minute now, so …

—Really? That's funny. He goes out every Wednesday at two and doesn't come back till four.

—How do you know that?

—Oh, just let's say I know. You see, it's my business to know these things, to notice these things.

—If you want a book that's fine. If not, please … leave.

—Lookit, there's no need to be hostile, Karen. I just want to ask you a few questions.

—What gives you the right to ask questions here? You're not a Japanese policeman.

He grinned, throwing his arms into the air.

—Next best thing.

I began to feel very uneasy and considered forcing him out of the store in some way and locking the door until Nakano-san returned. If this had happened a few months earlier I would have been intimidated into silence. But I now was not afraid to speak up.

—Look, why don't …

—Sh, baby, sh. Calm yourself down, will ya? Remember Chuck, the tall kind of hayseed-type guy? Sure ya do. Well, Chuck and me is military police. It's our job to make sure everything is, you know, on the up and up. So …

He walked forward until he stood at arms' length from me.

— … so, I thought you said you broke up with him. Now don't go sayin' "Who?" Y'all know who I mean. Eric. Eric Smith. He sort of stands out, if you know what I mean.

—I think you should leave right now. It is none of your …

—Oh yes it is my business, honey.

—Don't you call me that. Get the hell out of here!

—Sorry. It's just a quaint southern custom. We saw him leaving the bookstore last Sunday night. That's hours after your little bookstore closes. Quite the bookworm, is he? No, I think it's something far more, you know, I mean, tempting that's getting him to worm his way in.

—Get out of here right now!

—Lookit, Karen, you just hold your temper, okay? Gettin' all riled up is gonna get neither of us nowhere. This is very serious business here. Your Eric is involved with people on the base and stationed in 'Nam who are conducting anti-American activities. Were you aware of that?

—He is not. Eric would have nothing to do with that.

—No? Did he tell you about Tony Roberts? I can see that he hasn't. His bosom buddy, Tony, who shared a room with him at Zama, went to 'Nam and fragged a lieutenant in his bunk? Don't ring no bell? Know what that is, fragging? I can see that you don't. It's tossing a grenade at an officer, like when they're asleep. Well, next time you see your Eric, ask him about Tony Roberts and what happened to him. Lookit. Chuck and I are genuinely concerned about you. Hell, we know you've done nothin' wrong. You're just an innocent little girl who's gettin' way over her little old head. We just, you see, we just, I mean, we don't want you falling into the wrong hands. We don't want the wrong hands gettin' all over you.

—What is that supposed to mean?

—Mean? We followed Eric back to the base on Sunday night. We were in the same train car. He's obviously a very disturbed, you know, confused man. We wouldn't want a nice girl like you getting, you know, tainted, you know, tarred with the same brush, if you know what I mean. A girl like you.

—Eric has done nothing wrong.

He threw his arms into the air again.

—Hey, who's sayin' he has? Not yet at least. It's what he *might* do, that's my job to find out before he does it. There's a war on, you know, and it's on not only in 'Nam and here. It's on in every corner of the goddamn world. We gotta keep all those corners covered if we're gonna, you know, I mean, if America is gonna be strong to be able to do it.

—I don't follow. Now, I told you to get out and I mean it. It's not America here. You have overstayed your welcome in this bookstore.

—Overstayed my welcome? What kind of a highfallutin' thing is that to say? Don't get confused yourself, honey. It's not becoming. I don't take lightly to girls who're not becoming.

He put his hand out to shake mine. I just squinted, staring straight at him.

—Okay, I get it, Karen-san. No offense. No offense intended.

He pulled his hand in, shook his fingers, blowing on them as if they were burnt, started humming again and turned to go. I clenched my fists and bit down on my lower lip. I would have to warn Eric to stay clear of the two MPs. He opened the door and, holding on to the knob, twisted his head around toward me.

—Funny, you wouldn't know it by his name. Eric Smith. Most of them have, you know, more fancy handles, like Roosevelt F. Jackson the Third or somethin' like that. Anyways, y'all tell your friend, Private Smith, to keep his big black ass clean. Toodeloo, honey.

The bell over the front door rang and he was gone. I swivelled around, grabbing hold of the protruding edge of the counter, shut my eyes tight, bit down hard on my lower lip and said "dammit, dammit" over and over again. In the past I would have broken into tears out of a feeling of helplessness. But now I felt anger mixed with the overwhelming urge to protect Eric at all costs.

That realization helped me understand, maybe for the first time in my life, that I had finally grown up, daddy. Nothing mattered to me ... not my past, with its never-ending sunny days lying on my stomach on terrycloth beach towels and observing every tanned body that walked by me, not mom or you or even Jeff, not even my own safety. What I was terrified of before was the unknown. Everything that was going to happen to me was laid out before me. I could see my whole life stretched out in front of me ... and myself on the sidelines of it all. Me on the sidelines of my own life. But that was all *before*. Everything was different now. Not being able to foresee what was going to happen to me and not fearing it either gave me strength, and that strength was what I would use to protect Eric. Keeping him from becoming a man who killed others was the way I was going to save myself.

The bell above the front door rang again. I let go of my grip on the counter, sure that he had come back to taunt me.

—Karen-san?

—Oh, Nakano-san. Hello. I'm so glad it's you, I mean, that you've come back. But aren't you early?

—Yes. I was meeting with Hiromasa, but he had to leave early.

—How is he?

—He is very healthy, thanks to you. Oh, that is such a bad Japanese habit. We Japanese always say "thanks to you" even when something is not thanks to you. Have there been customers?

—Uh, no one buying anything.

—Hiromasa is going back to his university studies.

—Oh. So, what does he want me to do with his helmet and *gevabo*?

—Are they still with you?

—Yes. He left them in my room.

—Oh, that is *keshikaran*.

—What?

—Oh sorry. Just a moment. I always have my dictionary in my pocket. Yes. It is "outrageous, unpar ... unpardon ..."

—Unpardonable?

—Yes, that's it. Oh, English is too difficult.

—Does that mean that Hiro is no longer in the student movement?

—Yes, that's correct. He said to me, "Uncle, all I want now is to wear a suit and have a *meishi*, a namecard, from a big Japanese company, like Mitsubishi or something, with my name on it. Then when I meet people I can bow, hand to them my name card and without saying my name, just say, 'I am with Mitsubishi.'" He is trading in his big stick for a little card. It's much lighter.

—I feel like saying that's a shame, but maybe it isn't.

—Oh, no shame. You see, his heart was never in it, do you say?

—Yes.

—I think he joined the student movement because he loves Emiko. No, not just loves. He *suhai* her. Just a moment please. He "adores" her. He "worships" her. Do I say that?

—I understand.

—Anyway, as his uncle I support him whatever he becomes, even if he gives his heart to Mitsubishi. It is his life, not mine.

—Yes, his life. I see that.

A customer, the first of the afternoon, came into the store, followed by three others. The last hours of business turned out to be quite busy, allowing me, if only briefly, to take my mind off the anger and dread I was feeling. By evening this anger and dread had turned to revulsion. What did I have in common with those two American soldiers? Not a single thing, save for us having been born in the same country. I'd rather live my entire life somewhere else if it meant that I would never have to come into contact with men like them.

We closed the shop at six. Nakano-san left shortly after that. I stayed downstairs to be close to the phone. Not that I could tell

Eric about the MP's visit. That would have to wait till Saturday when I saw him. I now feared that someone was listening in to our phone conversations. What if the MP had gone back to the base and confronted Eric? "Your little white girlfriend, Karen-san, told us all about it. She knows what kind of people you've been associating with and wants nothing more to do with you. So, my friend, keep your filthy hands off her, will you? You go near her again and we'll have you up for some charge, I can promise you that. American servicemen like you are scum, and you will be treated like scum. Skimmed off the top and disposed of somewhere where no one will bother about you ever again." These were the words, *his* words, racing through my mind. My heart was pounding so hard I could feel my eardrums reverberating. Oh my God, no, he wouldn't say such things to Eric. That would be a stupid thing to do. He will bide his time and wait until Eric does something, makes an innocent mistake, and then come down on him like a ton of bricks. I was dying to tell Eric that we must not be there when those bricks come out of the sky like bombs to tear us apart and bury us.

The phone rang at ten to seven. I was standing right beside it and picked it up after only one ring.

—You're early. Oh, I need to talk to you so much.

—Hello, Karen?

—Hello?

—Hello? Karen? This is Dr. Rush, Ben Rush.

—Oh sorry. I was expecting a call. I'm sorry.

—What? Uh, are you well? Are you faring well?

—Yes, I'm fine, thank you. How are Jeannie and Fran, and how is Mrs. Rush?

—Oh, everyone's hunky-dory. Jeannie has a new boyfriend, but he's really nice. Fran is, well, you know, half a little child and half a young woman, and I don't think either side knows how to deal with the other.

—And Mrs. Rush?

—Oh, Ethel's fine. She's discovered Japanese flower arranging. It's her new "thing," as they say now. The wives meet twice a week with a Japanese lady who teaches them. You wouldn't recognize the house, Karen. It looks like we've got a little version of the Huntington Library garden in our own living room. So, when are we going to see you again? It seems like ages.

—Oh, I'll try to, I mean, I want to go. But work at the bookstore and studying Japanese every night, you know how it is.

—Sure. I wish my girls had your sticktoitiveness, I'll tell you that.

—Uh, Dr. Ben?

—What is it?

—Do you mind awfully? I'm sort of expecting a call now and, if you don't …

—Oh, sorry. Sure. Just one more thing, actually.

—Yes?

—Um, a Japanese policeman came to the house this morning before I went to work. He was asking about you.

—About me?

—Yes. Oh, I think it was just routine stuff. They check up on *gaijin* from time to time. It's a Japanese custom. Politest people in the world, but their politeness masks a deep suspicion of us. You can't take anything at face value with these people.

—I haven't found that, but….

—But what? You don't encounter it until you go deep into things here. Most foreigners just skim the surface, like rocks skipping on top of a lake, you know, bouncing merrily from one place to another without ever sinking in. They never get to know the Japanese the way they really are. These people are not really friendly and frank like we Americans are, Karen. Not deep down, where it counts.

—I see. Uh, Dr. Ben, I …

—I know. Sorry. Just another minute and I'll let you go. I told him, the policeman, that you were still living with us but that you had gone to stay with a Japanese girlfriend for a while to get a glimpse of what the real Japan was like. After all, Tachikawa here isn't really Japan, is it. But, Karen, I think they already know where you are because he made a mention of that place you are working in.

—Jinbocho?

—Yes, that's it.

—But how could they know that?

—I have no idea. They know a lot about foreigners, Karen. We stand out like sore thumbs here. I told him you aren't working there per se, that you were very studious and spent a lot of time at old bookstores. At any rate, I think you ought to come back to live here. I have spoken with the dean again and they are still happy to have you back. They said you can make up the lost time, but they said that you can't stay away much longer, because then they'll have to suspend you and notify U.S.C. that you've dropped out.

—I see.

—Finally, uh, sorry, this is the last thing. It's your dad.

—Is he okay?

—Yes. He's completely back on his feet, but he's naturally worried about you. After all, think about it, Karen. He's lost his wife and his son. You're all he has left in the world.

—I should write him, but I don't know what to say.

—Just let him know you're well. And remember, Karen, we consider you a member of the Rush family. You're welcome back here whenever you wish.

—Thank you, Dr. Ben. I appreciate it.

—Well, goodbye, then.

—Goodbye. Please say hello from me to Jeannie and Fran.

—Will do. Bye.

—Bye.

Did you register all of that, daddy? A few things may have passed you by, but you heard what Ben Rush said about me, didn't you? "You're all he has left in the world." That's why I've come back to you now. Everything else that you have, all your money and blue-chip stocks, your "units" in Downey, your sterling reputation as a physician, the pride you have in your country that you never cease telling everybody about … all of that has slipped out of your grip, daddy. You can't hold on to any of it. You can't move a muscle. You can't even make a decent fist anymore. You can't raise your voice and threaten anyone. So I guess that I am the only thing you do have left in the world. I am your medium. I am your sole mouthpiece. Only through me can you communicate with the world now.

If you could open your eyes right now and see me sitting at your bedside, what would you say to me? What would you do to me? Would you say, "Why are you being so cruel to me when I'm dying?" Would you slide over to me and slap me in the face like you did when I told you that Jeff hated you, that he left the country mainly to get away from you, from you, daddy, from YOU? You called Jeff a coward to his face. He said, "Yes, father, I am a coward. I want to be a coward. Force without wisdom collapses of its own weight, dad. You know that, don't you? You've studied ancient Rome. Look at your own country and learn!" Oh, your son was a wise young man, daddy, and you never knew it. You never found out. It was you who sent him away. He couldn't live in the same country as you, let alone under the same roof. So that's right. Now I am all you have left in the world. But remember. It's the world you created for yourself.

Eric didn't phone until nearly nine.

—I'm sorry being late, baby.

—I've been waiting by the phone dying of worry.

—I'm sorry. Look, I'm sorry, okay? There was a meeting I couldn't get out of.

—A meeting?

—Uh, look, it's nothing. Just some of us guys.

—Uh-huh.

—Is something wrong?

—No, Eric, I'm just tired, that's all.

—Well, get your beauty sleep because I'm seeing you on Saturday.

—And Eric? Hello, Eric?

—Yeah, I'm here.

—When you come, bring just a few extra things.

—What do you mean extra things?

—Oh, like a toothbrush and an extra sweater and some socks and stuff, you know.

—What are you planning, baby? We're not going hiking or anything like that, are we? I'm not into that, not after Scotland.

—No, just do it please.

—You really sound sort of, I don't know, grumpy or something.

—I'm not grumpy! I'm just tired, that's all. I haven't had dinner. I haven't even been up to my room since we closed.

—It's all my fault. Jesus, I'm really sorry. I'll explain everything when I see you.

I went to bed without eating. On Thursday I felt nauseous and sick in my joints, and I asked Nakano-san if I could stay in my room that day. By the next day I was feeling a lot better, though still a little nauseous. All I needed was a good walk in the brisk air. I took the subway to Yurakucho and made my way to the big intersection on the Ginza in the evening, entering the new Sony Building where the latest radios and tape recorders were on display.

—What do you think? Pretty sleek, no?

—I beg your pardon?

An elderly American couple, each with a Nikon F single-lens reflex camera suspended on a thick cloth strap from their neck, was standing in front of the latest model tape recorder.

—A darn sight better than we can make. You're American, aren't you? Where you from? We're from Pennsylvania.

—Uh no, actually. English.

The woman gently slapped her husband's arm.

—Jim, not everyone's American. I'm sorry, young lady, Jim makes it a habit of talking to Americans, I mean to people, when we're abroad. This is our fourth visit to Japan. We just love it here. So, where are you from in England?

—Uh, Oxford.

—Oh, Oxford! We went there. It's so, I mean, full of, you know, tradition.

—Excuse me. I've got to meet someone.

—Sure. TTFN.

—What?

—TTFN. Ta ta for now. Learned it in your country. The war. Guess you're too young for that sort of thing.

I went into Pub Cardinal on the first floor of the building, ordered a beer and sat over it for an hour. What if I had been born in a different country … would I be the same person I am now? Did I really want to be like a Japanese and live here all my life? What sort of future could there be for Eric and me in a country like this? No, I couldn't stay in Japan forever, I knew that. But could I go back to America? Was it because of Eric or myself that I was having those thoughts? Maybe there was more left of my country in me than I thought.

—So, here's my toothbrush and here's the socks and the extra sweater, a baby-blue alpaca Pringle sweater no less, bought in Glasgow. I was sweating bullets in the train with this thing on over my pullover.

He lifted the sweater over his head and threw it onto the tatami.

—I even brought a parka that I wore when Gordon and I were on top of the mountain in Glencoe. I haven't been on a mountain since, baby, but if it's what you want, I'm game. I'm going to be the best-dressed dude on the top of Mt. Fuji.

—It's not for hiking, sweetheart.

—No? What for, then? I'm not giving this stuff to the Salvation Army, if that's what you've got in mind.

—No, Eric. It's for you.

—For me?

—You might have to go on the run for a while.

—Don't bring that up, baby. You know I don't want things to go …

—You may not want things to go that far, but they might, Eric. You've got to be realistic. If you bring a few items each time you come to see me, it won't look suspicious and you'll have everything you need when the time comes.

—Suspicious? What are you talking about?

—There's this guy. I think his name is Frank.

—Don't know any Franks.

—He knows you.

—So?

—He followed you, together with the other MP.

—MP? How do you know that? They don't dress in uniform off base.

—He told me. They were on the same train as you. Did you see them?

—Hell, baby, every time I get on that Odakyu train from

Shinjuku on a Sunday night the cars are crawling with American soldiers, most of them zonked out of their gourds.

—These guys weren't zonked. They know who you are.

—Look, baby, that doesn't faze me. It's their job to keep tabs on us.

—Who is Tony Roberts?

He now stared me straight in the eye.

—How do you know about Tony?

—Why didn't you tell me about him?

Eric moved around the table, drumming his fingers on it as he walked.

—He didn't want to, I mean, to fight, to kill people so … so he took the only way out he could.

—Killing an officer?

—He didn't kill an officer. He threw a grenade into his bunk.

—Oh, that's not killing?

—Listen to me, Karen! You're not listening. He threw it in and pulled the pin. But he knew it was a dud. It was a grenade that had been rejected. Tony worked in ordnance. He knew what he was doing. He knew it wouldn't explode. But he hollered, "Sir, wake up, there's a grenade on your balls!" The dude, who by the way was an absolute shit, woke up, saw the grenade and nearly had a heart attack. But nothing happened to that officer. He just got scared shitless. They threw the book at Tony, though, to make an example of him. Tony was hauled before a military tribunal. They shoved him in the clink. Two years, baby, in Fort Leavenworth.

—Where's that?

—Kansas. Only no Wizard of Oz is going get you out of there. But you know, baby, he's happy. He wrote me a letter I got last week and said he felt freer there than in the army. Everyone has his own different prison, I guess.

—What are you going to do about this Frank guy?

—Let him follow me.

—But he knows about me.

—Since when is it a crime to be with your girl?

I walked around the table and put my arms around him.

—To some people it may be. It just makes them hate you more. That's what bothers me the most.

He kissed me, rubbing the small of my back.

—You worry too much, that's your problem. Hang loose, baby. Don't be such a worry bird. Things will work out.

I didn't understand Eric. One minute he was reduced to tears, telling me he couldn't imagine himself in Vietnam forced to watch people being tortured and killed, and the next he was telling me to "hang loose." When the time came to make a decision, maybe I was the one who would have to make it for him … and for me.

The next week Emi was arrested. The police had raided her apartment and found about two dozen empty sake bottles, gasoline, engine oil, kerosene and wads of cloth to make Molotov cocktails.

—They are keeping her in detention for questioning.

—Can anyone visit her, Nakano-san? I could go and bring her some …

—No. Absolutely not. Anyone who visits will be considered suspicious. In Japan there is no line between the victimizer and the victim. Touch a guilty person and you become guilty, even if it is just by chance. No one can go to her.

—What will she do?

—There is nothing that she can do. They can keep her for a long time without, how do you say, charging? They are free to find out what she knows.

—It's good that Hiro wasn't there with her.

—Yes. Hiromasa has abandoned the movement. They

searched the room where he lives, but they found nothing. It is good that you have his helmet and *gevabo*. But we must get them out of there, because the police may come to search your room. I will take them away for you.

—Thank you, Nakano-san.

—One more thing, Karen-san.

—What is it?

—Do you intend to go on keeping company, do you say, with Eric-san?

—Why do you ask? Do you object?

—Object? Not at all. But do you remember those two Japanese policemen who came here?

—Yes.

—They came back last Friday evening. You were out.

—They didn't go up to the room, did they?

—Oh no. But they said, "Your *gaijin* young lady is white and she has a *koibito*, a lover, who is a *kokujin*, a black man."

—What's it to them? It's none of their business.

—It is their business because they think it is. They are more prejudiced than Americans, Karen-san. Japanese people are worse than Americans. They are so quiet and polite and formal, but underneath they are mean and full of hate for people of other races. Before the war it was all right to say so. Now people don't say so. But they think so. If you marry Eric-san and have a baby, the baby will be two races. Japanese people do not understand people with two races. If they did, they wouldn't be able to think of themselves as pure. Please leave Japan someday, Karen-san. Perhaps we will be more tolerant in the next generation, in the 1990s or the next century, I don't know, it's too far away and I will not be living. But this is no country for you. Japan is no country where you can be yourself.

—I don't know anything anymore, Nakano-san. I am so confused. Where does a person belong?

—People belong where they can feel free to be themselves.

—I understand that. But first you have to know what it means to be yourself.

Nakano-san smiled, raising his index finger.

—Ah, yes. That is the hard one. In Japanese we call it *otona ni naru*, becoming an adult, growing up.

Eric had a huge beat-up knapsack on his back when he arrived on Saturday afternoon. He dropped it on my table and unzipped it.

—Okay, things for a rainy day, or should I say, for the gathering storm. Four Fruit of the Loom T-shirts and five pairs of Fruit of the Loom undies, six pairs of stretch socks in black and charcoal gray and, behold, a pair of gen-u-wine argyle socks from Gimbels Department Store in New York City. And, one suit bought for me by a very special lady. Now, that's not all. A suitably faded pendleton, never worn Levis and a pair of Spalding sneakers. I haven't forgotten my old Boy Scout oath. Be prepared.

—Why don't you get dressed in some of this stuff and take me out tonight? It's my treat.

—You're always treating me.

—Does it take away your manhood?

—Hmm, I don't know. Why don't you try me out and see?

He pulled me to him, lifted me up and laid me down on top of the futon. He was so full of passion, daddy, I lost myself in him. After we made love, we put the futon cover over us, hugged and kept kissing each other over and over.

Eric dressed in his Levis, pendleton, alpaca sweater and parka, and I put on the green floral cotton shirtwaister that I hadn't worn since Thanksgiving, a woollen pullover and my duffel coat. We went to the Ginza. We walked past the Sony Building and the Jena Bookstore in the direction of Mitsukoshi

Department Store.

—Wow, baby, it's just like we're on a honeymoon here, not two people on the run.

—Are we on the run?

—Well, I didn't mean it like that. I just meant sort of, you know, up in the air. Floating like a balloon, waiting for a wind to rise and take us in one direction or another.

We stopped in front of the Mikimoto Pearl store.

—Geemonelly, will you look at that brooch. That pearl's as big as a friggin' grape. Oh how I'd like to see that pinned to your beautiful chest.

—Look at the beautiful price, though. 3,800,000 yen. We're not Bonnie and Clyde, you know.

—A mere pittance, baby. It's, let's see, a bit over $10,000. I could make that in a couple of months running my dad's stores.

—Don't turn around, Eric.

—What?

—Shh. I just said don't turn around. Stay like this, looking into the window.

There were about half a dozen young American men with crewcuts coming up from a staircase in the building beside Mikimoto Pearl. They stopped on the sidewalk, no more than twenty feet from us, passed around a packet of Chesterfield cigarettes, lit up and looked around.

—What are they doing here?

—What? Who? What're you whispering for?

—I don't want them to hear. What are they doing here?

—Those guys? Guys like that go out all the time. There's a place on the Ginza where they kind of congregate. It's a club or something. Must be in that building.

Another group of crewcut men emerged from the building, each with a Japanese girl on his arm. Two of the girls broke away and ran up to us, standing right next to us at the window.

They clung to each other and remarked on how expensive the pearls were. Then, one of them turned to Eric.

—Hallo. You soldier? I like big black boys.

He smiled and shook his head.

—Nice jeans you got, black boy. I love.

—Thank you.

One of the Americans shouted to them.

—Hey, Etsuko, Nobuko, get your little asses over here, will ya? We're splitting.

The girls, still clinging to each other, ran toward the group. They all crossed the street, weaving in and out of traffic, in the direction of Yurakucho Station.

—See, you could have had a Japanese girlfriend too, if you wanted.

—I do have a Japanese girlfriend, baby. It's you. I've got the best of both worlds.

—Or the worst of both worlds.

—Now who's the one feeling sorry for herself.

Eric grabbed me and we ran toward the Sony Building. I took him to Pub Cardinal, where he ordered steak and kidney pie for both of us. Eric had been to England. If we ended up living there or somewhere else in Europe, he'd be the one guiding me.

It was the second week in April, the 11th to be exact. There is no way I will ever forget that day. Eric showed up at the bookstore, though it was a Thursday.

—What are you doing here? Are you allowed to leave the base today?

—Yes. I got leave this afternoon, said I had to go to the funeral of a friend's father. They raised an eyebrow but let me go. I have to be back tonight, though. I can't stay.

—Okay. Just a sec. I'll ask Nakano-san if I can take an hour off.

—Just a minute, baby. Dr. King died. He was assassinated last week.

—Yes, I know. I heard it on NHK radio. I'm sorry.

—I guess there'll be no more riots in Watts now.

—Yeah, now that the guy who started it all is dead.

—Are you kidding?

He closed one eye and furrowed his brow.

—Eric, what do you take me for? I'm being sarcastic. I'm a grownup. Finally. Can't you tell?

We went to the coffee shop next to Nauka, the Russian bookstore. It was the first time we had been there since we met. The same rugs were hanging on the walls, and balalaika music was coming out of the two speakers in the corner.

—I can't believe, like, half a year has gone just like that. So much has happened. When we were here before, you ordered coffee in Japanese and, like wow, I was so impressed.

The same man, the manager, who was there half a year earlier, came to our table in his Russian shirt.

—*Hisashiburi desu.* (It's been a long time.)

Though he was looking at Eric, I replied.

—*So desu ne. Kohi futatsu onegai shimasu.* (Yes, it has. We'll have two coffees, please.)

Eric took my hand and rubbed my knuckles.

—My Japanese girl.

—Yeah. So, sweetheart, really, what's up?

He let go of my hand and lowered his gaze.

—The day of reckoning, baby, that's why I'm here.

—What do you mean?

—Last night we got our marching orders. On Monday we transfer over to Yokota where they got the 610th.

—What's that?

—The 610th Military Airlift Support Squadron. They're the ones flying B-52s in and out of Vietnam. On Tuesday next, yours truly, Private First Class Eric Smith, is going to be sittin' in one of those mothers bound for Saigon.

—Oh my God. Eric. No.

—Now, look, don't cry. Look, coffee's coming.

The manager put a tray on our table, gave us our coffees and placed a small plate with two cookies on it between us.

—*Sabisu desu. Otomiiru kukki. Natsukashii desho.*

He sucked in air between his teeth, scratched the nape of his neck and walked away.

—These look like oatmeal cookies.

—They are. He said they're oatmeal cookies and they're free of charge. And he said, "I bet these take you back home."

Eric bit into one of the cookies.

—Jesus, it's the real thing. How come they got these things here?

—They've got everything American in Japan, except a real hamburger. You can't get one of those.

—Won't be long, I bet, till you can. They'll probably open a McDonald's on the Ginza or somewhere.

—I used to sell these cookies on my front lawn when I was in the Girl Scouts.

—You were in the Girl Scouts?

—Yes. What's so funny?

—Don't know. Just can't picture it. You seem, I don't know, different. Not the goodie-two-shoes type, that's all.

—I was, Eric. I was daddy's little girl. All the way. But listen, what are we going to do?

—I was trying to get my mind off it. Damned if I know. Maybe I'll just go and tough it out. Maybe I'll come home with a medal. How would that be, eh? You with your pearl brooch on your chest and me with my Purple Heart. Nice color combination, wouldn't you say? Deep purple and pearl white.

—Stop it, Eric. Maybe you'll come home in a wheelchair,

paralyzed from the waist down.

—I know, baby. I've seen guys. Would you still love me?

I picked up a cookie, but immediately put it down.

—Yes, I would.

—I wouldn't let you. I'd turn myself into such an ogre, such a horrible brutal beast that you'd be forced to leave me. "Oh, Eric used to be so sweet and considerate, now all he does is scream and cry, scream and cry." I've seen it. It happens to the best of them, baby. But what choice do I have?

—You could hide. We could hide until …

— … until they catch me … and you, too. They'll send me to Leavenworth and you'd be on that plane to L.A. quick smart. Home to daddy.

—Then I'd wait for you. Till you came out.

—Yeah, how long? Two years? Five years? Your daddy will introduce you to some good-looking young intern. He'll whisk you off your feet in his Corvette and promise you the world. What girl would choose a black good-for-nothing with a dishonorable discharge over that? No veteran's benefits, no nothing.

—Me. I would. Who needs benefits? When my father dies I inherit a fortune.

—Sounds nice, but Karen, it's not on. A girl like you waiting for a deserter out of Leavenworth? And if we did try to escape, do you really think they wouldn't find us? The first place they'd look for me is your room up there at the bookstore. What's his name, Frank? He'd be on us like the creature from the black lagoon. Those guys can make themselves invisible, baby. You don't see them until they're right on top of you and, bam! you're a dead duck, plucked right out of the water. If I went to live with you, they'd cotton on before we knew which end was up.

—There's another place. I've even been there to see it. It's off the beaten track for those MPs. No one knows about it. It's

Nakano-san's old place. It'll be safe. We could stay there. You wouldn't even have to go out. I'll do the shopping and stuff. Then Nakano-san will get you out of Japan.

—And after that?

—They will get you to Sweden, where you'll be safe. I will join you, I promise. The minute I know you're there I'll do whatever I have to do to be with you.

—And after that?

—After that … we live.

—And do what?

—I don't know, Eric! We live. That sounds good enough to me.

—Shh. Okay, I'm sorry.

—Just come back to the store with me now.

—I really don't have the time. People will start wondering why the funeral took so long.

—We need to talk with Nakano-san. We need to get you off the base before Monday. There's no two ways about it.

—No two ways?

—No. There's only one way. Only one way left to us.

Eric nodded, taking my hands in his and rubbing my fingers.

—Okay, baby, okay. If you say so.

Nakano-san seemed to be expecting this news from us. The moment I told him that Eric was ready to leave the base and go into hiding, he pulled us into the storeroom and shut the door.

—Listen carefully please, Eric-san. Do not come here on Sunday, but go instead to Yurakucho Station. Do you know it? It is between Tokyo Station and Shinbashi Station. Arrive there around noon. Walk all the streets, in and out, go into stores, up elevators, down and out another door, then finally make your way at two o'clock in the afternoon to the German Bakery. It is a restaurant beside Yurakucho Station. You go there separately,

Karen-san.

—Will you be there?

—No, I will not. You will be met and told what to do and where to go. Do you still have the key to my house at Nakarokugo?

—Yes. I went to see it. I got lost a bit, but I finally found it. I know where it is.

—Oh, you have much *senken no mei*. Just a moment please, I will check. "Foresight. The ability to see into the future."

—Do I? All I see ahead of us is a thick gray fog as far as the eye can see.

—That is good, because once you go through the fog you will at some time come out on the other side where the sun will be shining.

Eric put his hand on Nakano-san's shoulder and gripped it.

—I hope so, Mr. Nakano. But how long will we have to be in that fog before we get out?

On Sunday afternoon I packed my old valise and stuffed my purse with as many little things as would fit in it. I took the helmet and *gevabo* downstairs, stopping on the stairs to check if anyone was in the store. There were two customers browsing. One, a Japanese, left immediately, but the other, a Western man in his late twenties or early thirties, was hanging around the section on landscaping and gardening, gazing around from time to time. Nakano-san walked up to him and started conversing with him, before escorting him to the door and pointing in the direction of other English-language bookstores down the street. After the man left, I descended the stairs. I handed the helmet and *gevabo* to Nakano-san, who took them immediately into the storeroom. I returned to my room and came back down with my valise.

—*Nakano-san, nagai aida osewa ni narimashita.* (Nakano-san, you have helped me so much for a long time.)

He bowed to me and spoke English.

—You are the most wonderful person, Karen-san. I have watched you since December last year. You have changed. But one thing that has not changed and I think will never change. You have a very kind heart. Please do not lose it. Whatever happens to you, do not lose it and you will be okay.

I closed the shop door, listening for the bell as if it would be the last time I would hear it. I turned back to look through the window. Nakano-san was standing at the counter, staring out the window with a blank expression on his face. I looked up at the branches of the gingko trees lining the street. They were starting to sprout fresh green leaves. I took a deep breath as I gazed up at them and said to myself, "Well, here goes nothing."

I arrived at the German Bakery at five minutes to two. Three young Japanese women in light-blue uniforms stood behind a long glass-fronted counter that displayed a variety of fancy Western cakes and pies. They glanced toward the door when I walked in and shouted in unison.

—*Irasshaimase*! (Welcome!)

In the far corner of the room I caught sight of Iwabuchi-san, his hands folded on the table and his brown felt hat beside them.

—*Konnichiwa*. (Hello.)

—Please let us speak English. It is better here.

I sat down, putting my valise next to my chair and my purse on top of it.

—Sure. I understand.

—Where is he?

—I don't know. I'm sure he'll come.

One of the young waitresses from behind the counter came up to our table.

—*Gochumon wa okimari desho ka*? (Have you decided on your order?)

Iwabuchi-san told her that we were waiting for one other person and that we would order when he came.

Fifteen minutes passed and Eric had still not shown up.

—Shall I go and see if I can find him?

—No. He must come here. The station is very crowded and you will not find him.

Iwabuchi-san looked at his watch and fiddled with the brim of his hat.

—I will wait until 2:30 and then I will go.

—But what will we do then?

—I cannot wait longer. This is very dangerous.

The three waitresses were staring at us. An older man in a light-blue sport coat, white shirt and bowtie was now also serving customers. I bowed my head to the waitresses behind the counter and smiled, as if to say that it would just be a little longer before we ordered.

It was 2:30 and still no Eric. Iwabuchi-san took his hat in his hands.

—No, please, just wait ten minutes more. He must be having trouble finding it.

—I will wait five minutes. Only five minutes.

I stood and walked to the window, hoping to catch a glimpse of Eric nearby. The restaurant was now full, and there were several groups of people waiting by the entrance for a table. If he didn't come in the next five minutes, we would have to leave. The entire plan would have to be abandoned.

Iwabuchi-san stood up, put on his hat and picked up an old brown leather briefcase that I had not seen from beside his chair. He walked up to the counter and, bowing, said something to the waitresses, then made his way to the entrance. One of the women went to our table and put our untouched glasses of ice water on a tray, gazing down at my valise and purse. A young Japanese couple, who had been waiting at the entrance, approached the table and stood over it, preparing to sit down. Just then Eric, clutching his knapsack to his chest and panting as if he had been running, entered the restaurant.

—I'm sorry, baby, I had a hell of a time finding this damn place.

—It's right by the station, Eric!

—I know. But this is a hell of a long station, and I didn't know what side it was on. I ended up asking a policeman.

—You spoke with a policeman?

—What's the big deal? He was very nice.

I made a beeline to our table and plopped down in a chair just as the young Japanese man was pulling it out to sit down.

—*Sumimasen ga mada desu.* (I'm sorry but we're not finished.)

Iwabuchi-san returned from the entrance, put his hat on the table, sat down and beckoned Eric to come. The young couple returned to the entrance to wait for a free table. The three waitresses just stared at us without smiling. The man in the blue sport coat came to our table.

—*Sa, nani ni shimasho*? (So, what'll it be?)

Iwabuchi-san looked up at him.

—*Kohi mittsu.* (Three coffees.)

—*Sore dake desu ka*? (Is that all?)

—*Hai.* (Yes.)

He turned about and rushed back to the counter with the tray and ice water.

—You are late.

—I'm sorry, Iwabuchi-san, I …

—Do not use my name.

—I'm sorry.

—We have only a few minutes. I must leave. Listen very carefully please. Go to the Nakarokugo house of Mr. Nakano. Today is the 14th. You stay there, both of you, until Friday the

19th. She may leave the house to buy food, but you must not leave or be seen. Do you understand?

—Yes, sir.

—On Friday at 10 p.m. the Ordzonikidze leaves Yokohama Port for Nakhodka. You will find instructions on how you will get to the port at Mr. Nakano's house. Please study them carefully and then burn them. You must arrive at the Yokohama Port at the pier specified on the instructions by 9:30 p.m. at the latest. If you are not there by 9:30 you will not go on the ship and there will be nowhere for you to go. Do you understand?

—Yes, sir.

—And you?

—Yes I do, Iwabu … yes, I do.

—That is all.

He stood, produced a blank white envelope from his briefcase, put it on the table and pushed it toward Eric with his middle finger.

—Now, here is 30,000 yen in this envelope. This will be money for you until the 19th.

—But how do we get to Nakarokugo from here? By train?

—No, you must not be seen together in public. All Japanese notice you two when you are together. Take a taxi from the station now.

The Japanese man in the sport coat and bowtie brought a tray with three coffees on it to our table. Iwabuchi-san leaned down to us and whispered.

—You two go now.

Iwabuchi-san put a 500-yen note on the tray and walked out. Eric stood, picking up my valise.

—Let's go.

Everybody's eyes followed us from our table through the entrance and onto the street.

I could see that Eric was very nervous as we drove in heavy traffic south through the city.

—My palms are all clammy.

I put my palm against his.

—I like it when we have our hands like this. It's as if we can't be separated. As if your hands are my hands, connected to one body.

The driver was peering at us in the rear-view mirror.

—Much traffic. Soon Golden Week holiday so very busy, very very busy.

He turned his head around to smile at us.

—You American?

—Yes.

—Oh, so good. You know, I drive for Capt. Jenkins in Occupation. So many years ago. He such nice man. Give me many records. I still have. Tennessee Waltz, you know? Come On-a My House, you know? That's Rosemary Clooney. I love her so much. And Andrew Sisters. Andrew Sisters so cute, so good, you know?

He flashed a big smile, displaying a solid row of gold and silver capped teeth. We arrived at Kamata Station and I asked him to drive along the train line. When we were about a two-minute walk from the house I told him to stop.

—Here okay?

—Yes, thank you.

He stopped the car, got out, went around to the trunk and took my valise and Eric's knapsack out of it. After I paid him, he removed his cap and bowed low to us.

—Thanks awfully.

He put his hand out to Eric, who shook it, then to me. I shook his hand and thanked him. He again took his cap off, bowed, slammed the trunk shut, got into the driver's seat, closed his door and drove off.

For a moment Eric and I stood beside the tracks. We both sighed a deep sigh, no doubt thinking the same thing ... what's going to become of us ... is this adventure or folly ... would the five days holed up together in a little shabby house in a working-class suburb of Tokyo be our last time together ... and even if it all went to plan and Eric safely boarded the ship and made his way to the Soviet Union, would we really ever see each other again?

A long train passed us by, slowing down as it approached Kamata Station about a quarter of a mile down the track. Eric kissed me on the cheek and whispered in my ear.

—Come on. I can't wait to see our new home.

He picked up my valise. I slipped my arm under his as we crossed the tracks and turned the first corner into a narrow alley.

—It's almost like we're really on our honeymoon now, baby.

I leaned toward him on tiptoes and kissed him on the neck.

—Are you going to carry me over the threshold then?

—If that's what you want, baby, if that's what you want.

By Thursday night we felt as if we had been living there for an age.

—It would be nice though if we could go out together. I hate going shopping and thinking of you cooped up in here.

Eric kept fit by doing pushups, and I did my best to keep up with him, though when we did them together the whole little house shook.

—The family that sweats together stays together, baby.

—Well, it might be a bit more romantic if we had a shower here. If my father could see this place he'd have a cow. "Imagine someone from California living in a place without a shower," he'd say. "How primitive can you get?" I can hear his voice coming to me now.

—There's a bath here, though.

—Yes, there is. But it's way too small for you to get into, Eric. I saw you trying to squeeze into it on Tuesday night. Your knees were behind your ears.

He sat up and stretched his legs out on the tatami mat, crisscrossing them with mine.

—Here, wipe your face with this.

I threw him a small towel.

—Listen, baby, why don't we try and go out to dinner tonight? I bet there are some really good places right …

—No, Eric! You can't go out. We're leaving this house tomorrow night on our way to Yokohama. I'm taking no chances with you. You heard what Iwabuchi-san said.

—Okay, okay. What will you do after I leave tomorrow night?

—The instructions say, "Karen-san returns to Jinbocho room." I don't know how I'm going to get there from Yokohama so late. Maybe someone's going to drive me.

—Let me see those instructions one more time.

We unfolded the large piece of paper with the map and instructions on it.

The X on this map marks the Daikoku Dock (called DAIKOKU FUTOH in Japanese) Pier L-1. This is where you must go. Look at the map and memorize it and how to say it in Japanese.

Take the Keihin-Tohoku Line train from Kamata Station at 20:30 and get off at 20:54 at Kannai Station. From there take a taxi to Pier L-1 at Daikoku Dock. It is 6 kilometers distance from the station. When you arrive at the pier, do not stand under a lamppost. Go to the side. You will be met there. Karen-san returns to Jinbocho room.

Now put fire to this paper please.

We both said "Daikoku Futo" over and over again to make

sure we could pronounce it so that the cab driver would understand us. I had found a box of matches in a kitchen drawer the day before. I put the piece of paper on a plate and held it over a lighted match. We watched it shrivel in the flame and turn to ash.

—Could you clear these ashes up? I'm going out to get us something to eat.

—And a bottle of sake to celebrate?

—Sure, why not. I'm sure Iwabuchi-san wouldn't mind us using some of his money in a good cause.

As I stood up from the table, bent over and kissed Eric on the lips, there was a single knock at the door.

—Oh my God, who can that be?

—Must be Mr. Nakano. It couldn't …

There was another knock, louder than the one before.

—You better see who it is, baby.

I undid the little bolt in the door and slid it open.

—Emi!

—Can I come in?

—How did you know we were here?

—Nakano-san told Hiro. He told me.

—But I thought you and Hiro were …

—We're still friends.

She slipped past me, and I slid the door shut and locked it.

—Hi Eric.

—Hi.

—Emi, look, don't get me wrong, but maybe you shouldn't really come here.

—I needed to see Eric one more time. I know he is leaving tomorrow night.

I gestured for her to sit down.

—We thought you were arrested.

—I was. They questioned me for a few days, not letting me

sleep much. They wanted me to sign a confession and said if I did they would let me go.

—Did you sign?

—No, Eric, of course not. Why should I do anything for those fascist dogs?

I sat down. Eric picked up the plate with the pile of ashes on it and put it in the sink.

—What if they followed you here?

—They didn't, Karen. I was let go three days ago.

—They could be following you for those three days.

—I will leave soon, Karen. Don't get so excited. I have a letter for you to take, Eric.

—A letter?

—Yes. It is for our colleague in Moscow. He is an old Japanese communist who went to the Soviet Union before the war. During the war he was purged and sent to the Zona, but after the war they treated him like a comrade.

—What's the Zona?

—Oh, it means "the Zone." It's what the Russians call their labor camps. Here is the letter. Give it to Okada. He will contact you at your hotel in Moscow.

—What's in the letter, Emi?

—It is about the riot police here and how they gather intelligence. Someone in Moscow is helping them, I think. We need to find out who it is.

—Are you sure it's safe for me to take it?

—I think you should take it for Emi, Eric. She has put herself in such danger to get you out of Japan.

Eric picked up the envelope, putting it on his palm and moving his hand up and down, as if weighing it.

—It's only a piece of paper, but it feels like the weight of the world is in here.

—Thank you, Eric. And thank you so much, Karen-san. I

must leave now.

—We're going to have some dinner, if you …

—No, I can't stay.

I walked her to the front door. She turned toward me and threw her arms around me, hugging me tightly. This was the first time I had ever been hugged by a Japanese.

—I must admit, at first I did not appreciate you. I saw so many girls like you when I lived in L.A. All they cared about was their hairdos and who was going to go to the senior prom with jocks in lettermen's sweaters. You are different from that, Karen-san. I am sorry for being mean to you.

—No, Emi, you described the way I used to be to a T.

Emi left and I went to the grocery store to get food for dinner, locking the door behind me. Next door to the grocery was a liquor store, where I bought a bottle of Hakushika sake. When I got home, Eric was talking on the phone.

—Who is it?

He gestured for me not to speak.

—Who is it, Eric?

—Shh.

He hung up and sat at the table.

—It was Mr. Iwabuchi. He asked if we are ready for tomorrow.

—We are, aren't we?

—Sure, baby, sure. I told him that Emi had come here and he kind of blew his stack. What does *baka* mean?

—Idiot, fool.

—He kept hollering that word over and over when I told him Emi was here.

—Maybe he's worried that she was followed. That would ruin everything.

—I don't know, baby. Here, give me that bottle. Nakano-san has a little jug on the shelf there to heat it up. I'm going to miss this stuff. I wonder if we'll ever be together again in Japan.

Without Japan we would never have met each other.

—Maybe we'll come here again. Who knows? Maybe a couple like us will be able to live freely here and be accepted. In the future. When we get out of that fog.

I cooked a pancake called *okonomiyaki* in a frying pan and we drank half of the bottle of sake in tiny cups as we ate. At about nine we went into the bedroom. I opened a closet. Nakano-san's wife's dresses were hanging in it, and below them were her shoes in neat rows. We got into the double bed and cuddled up to each other and I thought … "This is our little world now, both of us from America, both so far away from home and on the run, yet feeling more ourselves than ever … and in one more day it could all be a thing of the past."

While I held myself as close as I could to Eric, daddy, and he didn't stop kissing me, I thought, "At least I have had this. Nobody can take this day and this night away from me." Not even you.

It was 7:30 on Friday evening. Everything was packed, and we were ready to go. Eric was wearing the charcoal gray suit I bought him on the Ginza. We sat in silence at the table below the naked light bulb. I rubbed the back of Eric's hand and smiled at him. He put his palm over my hand, leaned forward and kissed me. I could see a film of tears covering his eyes.

—You'll be all right, sweetheart. We'll be all right.

—I hope so.

—Oh, Nakano-san gave me a book to pass on to you. I put it in your knapsack.

—Yeah, I saw it. Richard Wright's "The Outsider." That's me, all right.

—Come on, Eric!

—Sorry. I know, a man's worst enemy … self-pity. It rivets

you to your seat. You can't budge. You just sit in your wretched little spot and wait until someone or something is right upon you like a, like a huge wave, and you think it's washed over you. But before you can get your feet planted again, it's carried you away with it. That becomes your direction in life, your fate. You suffer not for something you've done, but for lacking the courage to swim for once in your life against the tide.

—Eric, you do have courage.

—Do I?

—Yes. The courage to opt out of cruelty. I'm not going to sit and wait anymore either. I've let other people decide everything for me all my life and that's over. One time you are told that you are swimming against the tide, and years later you find that you were a small part of the new tide.

—You are so wise, Karen.

—Me? I never thought of myself as wise.

Eric stood, walked to the front window and peeked through the curtains.

—Hey, baby, come here for a minute.

—Wait a sec.

—No, come here.

I stood beside him and looked out.

—See those two guys across the street?

—Oh my gosh, they're the same two men who once came to the store to question Nakano-san. They're police, Eric. They know. They know we're here.

—Shit shit shit. They'll track us to the pier and I'll be caught there for sure.

—They couldn't know about that. Iwabuchi-san is too careful. We have to make sure they can't follow us.

—What if they caught Emi, though? They'd get it out of her that I was going on a Russian ship.

—Emi'd never tell. Never.

—What are we going to do?

—Let me think.

I walked back to the table and sat down, facing the kitchen sink. At the back of the kitchen there was a small entryway and a back door blocked by cardboard boxes piled one on top of the other.

—Eric. Eric!

—What?

—Get your knapsack and my valise. We're leaving.

—But it's too early, baby. We'll be spotted waiting at the station or arrive at the pier too early or something.

—Just get them. Do as I say.

I went to the back door and tried to move the boxes, but they were too heavy for me.

—Give me a hand here.

He came through the kitchen into the back entryway and lifted the top box a few inches.

—Jesus, what does he have in these things?

—Probably printed stuff. For demonstrations.

—Weighs a ton.

Together we moved the boxes into the kitchen. Eric put his knapsack on his back and picked up my valise. Leaving the light over the table on, we slipped out the back door, hopped over a low unpainted picket fence into a neighbor's backyard and walked through their garden into the back street. We went up to the corner and again went through someone's garden, back toward Nakano-san's street. I peered down it.

—Eric, come here, quick.

—What?

—Just stand flush against this concrete wall.

—What? Why?

—I can see the two policemen down the street. They're still waiting in front of the house.

—Yeah, but this here is a cul-de-sac. We can't get to the station without going past them. Even if we go down that other street, they'll still see us when we get to the corner.

I looked at my watch.

—We've still got time. Look, there's that church Nakano-san talked about. Follow me.

We crossed the narrow street and entered the Nakarokugo Lutheran Church.

—How do you think they found us?

—I don't know, sweetheart. They must've followed Emi.

—Yeah, must've been that. If they catch me with this letter in my knapsack, I'm a goner. They'll arrest me as some kind of Russian spy or something. That's all I need.

It took a minute for our eyes to get accustomed to the dim light in the church. We could see a man walking around the altar below a large round stained-glass window. He looked up.

—Hello?

—Hello. Excuse us. May we speak with you?

He walked up the aisle and stood before us, a man in his late seventies or early eighties with a shock of unkempt wiry white hair and bright blue eyes.

—Good evening. Oh, you must be Karen and Eric.

—You know us?

—Yes. Nakano-san has spoken about you for some time now. He is very fond of you both. I see you are going on a journey.

—Well, we didn't plan on coming here, sir.

—Please call me Joseph.

—Thank you. We were going to go to the station in a little while, but there are two men, policemen, in front of the house.

—I see. I am familiar with that from the wartime. I saw much worse then. This was my church even at that time, but I made sure that the police never entered here once. I gave safety to some Japanese who would not go to war then. But that will not do for you. You will be sought out by the Americans. They have special privileges in this country. I cannot stop them. What time must you leave?

—We have to be on an 8:30 train from Kamata Station.

—I see.

He glanced at his watch.

—Then I think we should be going.

—But how?

—In my Volkswagen Panel Van, of course. I have been to every corner of Japan in it and it has never let me down once. It is parked in the back. Come.

We went out the church by a side door and walked around to the back, where there was a garage with no door.

—In German it is a *hochdach*, a high-ceiling van. Very good for all sorts of purposes.

When we entered the garage I could see that the van was dark green. It had dents and rusted scratches on its sides and no windows in the back half.

—It's not very nice in there, but please get in. Your policemen will not see you in there.

We sat in the back seat. Eric put my valise on the seat beside him, placed his knapsack on top of it and leaned forward, resting his elbows on the back of the front seat.

—Just one thing before we go, if I may.

—Yes, Eric?

—I have a letter here which I cannot really take with me. If I do get caught with it, it would be dangerous for a lot of people. Would you please give it to Nakano-san? I'm sure he will know what to do with it.

He nodded and put out his hand. Eric unzipped his knapsack, removed the envelope that Emi had given him and handed it to Joseph.

—Thank you.

—Not at all.

—Why do you do this kind of thing for people? Do you mind my asking?

He turned the ignition key and the engine spluttered to a start.

—It's not because I am a man of the cloth, if that's what you mean. Many pastors and priests in Germany under the Nazis were only too happy to turn people in to the police and bless the SS.

—Then why?

He turned around and smiled at us.

—Why are you doing what you are doing, Eric?

—I don't know. I guess because I have been left with no other choice.

—That sounds very much like me too. Now, it's nearly ten after eight. We had better be on our way.

As he drove along the street, Eric and I ducked down until we had turned the corner and crossed the tracks. When we got to the station, he stopped the panel van by the main entrance and the three of us got out.

—I cannot thank you enough, Joseph.

He hugged Eric and then turned to me.

—Goodbye to both of you. Don't lose heart. Whatever happens, don't lose heart.

The station was bustling. Men on their way home from work were rushing out the exits. Buses with bright headlights on were careening into their stops, loading passengers and pulling out again. A line of cabs stretched all the way back to the side of the station, moving forward and picking up one passenger after another. We climbed the stairs into the station, bought two tickets to Kannai and handed them to the man punching tickets at the ticket gate.

—*Kannaiyuki wa nanbansen desu ka*? (Which is the platform

for the train to Kannai?)

He held up two fingers.

—*Nanba tsu.* (Number two.)

—*Arigato gozaimasu.* (Thank you.)

—*Don ma-in.* (Don't mind.)

The train pulled in just as we were descending the stairs to the platform.

—Just in the nick of time.

—We're fine, sweetheart. Everything is going to work out fine. Time is on our side.

—Yeah. Maybe for once it is.

We sat down. I looked around the train car, wondering if any of the people there could possibly be police. Men in dark suits with attache cases sat reading newspapers, and high school boys in black uniforms were chatting with each other and roaring with laughter. An old woman in a gray and biege checked kimono was perched on her knees on the seat, her *zori* slippers placed neatly beside each other on the floor below.

—I think we're okay, Eric.

—So far so good.

—These are just ordinary people.

—Yeah. In this car.

We arrived at Kannai Station precisely at 8:54. We stood at the door and were gently pushed out of the train by the crowd behind us. We waited on the platform until most of them had gone.

—What's the matter, baby?

—Oh, I was just lost for a sec. I never was on a train, not once, until I came to Japan. In L.A. you drive everywhere. But a person gets used to something new, some new kind of life, and it all becomes so matter of fact, as if this has been your life forever. But sometimes you flash back to your old self and you wonder if it's really you living this life.

—There's plenty of time for philosophy when we get ourselves out of this, baby. Let's get to that cab. I won't rest easy until I'm waving goodbye to you from that ship.

There was an even longer line of people waiting for cabs in Kannai than in Kamata.

—Oh my gosh, there are so many people. What if we're late?

—Shh, it'll be okay. There're enough cabs.

A flow of empty cabs kept coming in and throwing their back door open as passengers approached them. It was ten minutes past nine when Eric and I got into our cab. We had twenty minutes to get to the pier.

—*Sumimasen ga daigoku futo onegai shimasu.* (Please take us to Daigoku Futo.)

—*Daigoku Futo? Wakarimasen.* (Daigoku Futo? Don't know what you mean.)

—*Eeto, futo. Futo.* (Uh, the dack. Dack.)

—*Daigaku desu ka?* (You mean, the university?)

—*Ie, daigaku ja nai.* (No, not the university.)

—What's the matter?

—I don't know. He doesn't seem to understand my Japanese.

—Baby, we got only a few minutes. I thought you learned it. We've got to get there.

—I know!

The cab behind honked us and our driver was getting visibly irritated.

—*Betsu no takushi ni notte kudasai.* (Please take another taxi.)

—*Ie, sumimasen. Futo. Ano, fune ga deru tokoro.* (No, sorry. The dack. Um, where the ships go out from.)

—*Aa, fuTOH ka? Wakarimashita. Daikoku Futoh desho.* (Oh, the dock! I got it. Daikoku Dock, right?)

—*So desu. Hayaku onegai shimasu.* (That's right. Please go

quickly.)

He screeched out of the cab line and made a sharp U-turn onto the main street, then drove at a moderate speed through a built-up area. When we came to an almost deserted highway, he stepped on the gas pedal and we sped along. The sea came into view. I asked him to take us to Pier L-1. As we crossed a bridge linking piers, we could see about half a dozen big ships moored by them.

The driver pointed to enormous cranes lining one of the piers.

—*Koji desu. Konteina ga kondo kurun da.* (That's construction. Soon we're getting containers.)

—*Hai hai. Onegai shimasu.* (Yes, yes. Please.)

It was 9:35 when we arrived at Pier L-1. I saw a two-story building lit up by lamps on its outer walls about 100 yards ahead of us.

—*Koko de ii desu.* (Here is fine.)

The driver abruptly stopped the cab and the back door swung open.

—*Sen yonhyaku en.* (1,400 yen.)

I opened my purse. I had only one 10,000-yen bill, a 500-yen note and 60 yen in 10-yen coins. I handed him the 10,000-yen bill.

—*Otsuri nai desu yo. Komakai okane nai desu ka?* (I don't have change for this. Don't you have something smaller?)

I shook my head. He shut the back door and started driving toward the building.

—*Soko ni aru daro.* (They'd have it there.)

—Stop!

He screeched to a stop. I exchanged glances with Eric.

—*Ii desu.* (This is fine.)

He opened the back door again and we got out.

—*Otsuri do shimasho?* (What about the change?)

—*Ii desu. Irimasen.* (It's fine. I don't need it.)

The back door of the cab slammed shut, and the cab made a sharp U-turn, disappearing over the bridge between the piers. A big ship with Russian lettering on its prow was docked on the other side of the building. Just then a man appeared from the building, stood under the lamp over the entrance, looked at his watch and gazed around the area. His face was hidden in the shadow of the brim of his hat.

—It must be Iwabuchi-san. That's the same kind of hat he wears.

—I'll go up and see.

Eric put my valise down and walked toward the building. When he was halfway there he turned back to me and waved for me to come. Iwabuchi-san approached us in the dark.

—*Osoi desu.* (You're late.)

—*Gomen nasai.* (We're sorry.)

—*Ma, nantoka maniau daro.* (Well, you'll somehow make it.)

—What did he say?

—He said you're going to make it.

—Boy. You know, I feel just like those guys in the spy movies, except it's me and this is for real.

—Come this way, Eric-san. Karen-san, you go to the side of the building and wait for me. I will take you back to Jinbocho.

I hugged Eric, and we looked into each other's eyes.

—I will see you, baby. And I will be with you again in some city, wherever it is on the planet. Together, every night, we'll bury the sun there. Together, forever.

—I love you, Eric. I love you so much.

—I love you, Karen. Thanks to you, I'm no longer invisible.

—It's not thanks to me. It's you, Eric. It's thanks to you that I have come to see myself as I am and will be from now on.

He smiled his beautiful smile at me.

—*Hayaku. Jikan nai desu yo. Minna notteru yo.* (Quick.

There's no time. Everyone's on already.)

—Bye, baby.

—We've got all the time in the world now. Bye, sweetheart.

We walked together a few yards and separated when we reached the front of the building. As Eric and Iwabuchi-san headed for the ship, two men appeared as if out of nowhere. They took Eric by each arm. Iwabuchi-san stopped in his tracks and watched them walk toward the gangway, where three Japanese officials in uniform and caps were standing. Eric turned around, half lifting an arm to wave to me. But the two men, now staggering as if drunk, held tightly onto him.

I stood alone in the shadow of the building. When would I see Eric next? Was there a chance that I would never see him again? I had never felt such a sense of longing and heartache. I could still see his back, yet it was as if we had already been apart for days.

I heard the loud screech of tires. A black jeep sped from behind the building in the direction of the ship. Iwabuchi-san, the two men who held Eric's arms and Eric turned their heads at the sound. Eric and the two men ran for the gangway. They were stopped by the Japanese officials there. The jeep came to a halt behind them, the doors swung open and three men in American army uniforms jumped out. I dropped my valise and ran toward the ship, passing by Iwabuchi-san.

—Private Smith. Halt!

The two men let go of Eric's arms and bounded up the gangway. Eric tried to follow them, but the Japanese officials were blocking his way.

I could now see that the three Americans were MPs, and that two of them were Frank and Chuck. Frank went right up to Eric.

—You didn't think we'd let you get away, did you? You stupid fucking asshole.

Eric threw a desperate glance at me, shaking his head sharply, to tell me to stay away. Frank followed his gaze to me, flashing a big smile.

—Sure, Karen's come to see you off. The only trouble is, off to where? Military prison. That's where you're going, Sambo. We know everything, even the brand of *saki* your little white slut bought for you.

Eric raised his right arm and punched Frank in the jaw with great force. Frank fell straight back, hitting his head on the asphalt. His jaw dropped open and a mouthful of blood gushed out from between his lips. Chuck and the other MP grabbed Eric, threw his knapsack to the ground and put him in a half nelson, forcing his jaw against his chest. Frank stood, wobbling on his feet, picked up the knapsack, unzipped it and reached deep into its side pocket.

—Well, lookee here. What's this tobacco doing in this clear plastic bag?

He opened the plastic bag and smelled its contents.

—Uh-oh, it's not tobacco at all. It's maryjane. Well, Sambo, you're in deep shit now.

Eric shouted to me.

—That's not mine. Baby, that's not mine.

I whispered to myself.

—I know, Eric, I know!

—Well, it's in your bag and you were caught with it not only going AWOL but deserting. Snow White isn't gonna see your black ass for a long long time now, Sambo. What's that song, eh? Will you still love me when I'm sixty-four?

The two MPs shoved Eric into the car, one of them kicking him in the lower back as he got in. Frank, now holding Eric's knapsack, saluted me and blew me a kiss.

The jeep drove off in the direction of the bridge. Iwabuchi-san was still standing about fifteen yards from me, and behind him, lit by the lamps attached to the building, I could see my valise. The Japanese officials walked passed me as if I wasn't there. The gangway made a loud clanging noise as it was hauled up onto the ship.

I'm looking at the clock on the white wall, daddy. It's 5:27. I can see dim light coming through the curtains over the window in the room. I can hear people walking the corridor and speaking in muffled voices. In about half an hour Dr. Cohen will walk in as promised. "I'm never late," he said before he left last night. He'll ask about your "progress." I'll tell him that you have been breathing normally all night long. It's as close to the truth as I can get now. I'm going to the bathroom so just sit tight.

I went into the bathroom and turned on the light, squinting from its intense brightness. I lifted up the hem of my dress, pulled my undies down to my ankles and sat on the toilet. I put my head in my hands. I had been back in L.A. for six days. I had visited my father every day for about an hour. But this was the first time I had spent the night at his bedside.

I flushed the toilet, pulled up my undies, stood in front of the mirror on the medicine chest and stared at myself. It was the 6th of June, 1968, and the weather had turned hot. I had driven along Sunset Blvd. last night to the hospital on Fountain Ave., seeing kids barely sixteen driving big new convertible two-tone Cadillacs and silver Chrysler Imperials. I had waited at a light beside one kid whose spit curl barely came up to the steering wheel. An old man in a ten-year-old Plymouth had stopped next to him. He was a balding Eastern European-looking man, probably a refugee, in a tattered shirt and glasses that sat askew on his nose. He stared at the boy in his flashy car with profound disgust. Yet in what way was I different from that kid? I'm not that much older than him, driving my father's red Buick Invicta convertible. I'm living a life again here in L.A. that I have done nothing to earn or deserve. If the old man in the Plymouth had turned my way, he would no doubt have sneered at me with the very same degree of contempt.

I combed my fingers through my hair, straightened my dress and went back to my father's bedside. He had stopped breathing. I called to him … "Dad? Daddy?" But he didn't respond. How many minutes had he been like that? The clock said 5:33. I had been in the bathroom for six minutes … well enough for him to die. I didn't want to shake him. I was afraid I would dislodge one of the tubes or the catheter. I slapped him on the cheek. He still wouldn't breathe. I slapped his cheek twice again, harder. His jaw dropped open and he seemed to gasp for a breath, but only a single one. I looked around the room, as if someone might have come while I was in the bathroom. The cord of the call buzzer was draped over the arm of my chair on the other side of the bed. I called to him again, this time close to his ear … "Daddy, wake up! Daddy, it's me, Karen. Wake up!" His jaw dropped open again, and he took a deep breath, paused, then took another … and another. He started to breathe regularly again.

Does this mean that the end is near? Would he take one final long breath, let out all the air in his lungs and then stop breathing forever? Would I be responsible for his death, seeing as I could easily have pressed the button and summoned a nurse or, at this time of the morning, a doctor?

After Eric was arrested I returned to Tachikawa to live with the Rushes. Ethel had left Japan to look after her mother, Mrs. Duvall, who died in April, and had not yet come back to Tachikawa. This meant that Jeanette and Fran did all the cooking. I say "cooking," but they just went to the PX on Saturday and bought a week's worth of TV dinners, mostly fried chicken. Jeanette's new boyfriend, Bob, who she met on a beach in Okinawa, was back home in San Diego studying marine biology, but he had sent her his fraternity pin which she wore every day. Fran had put her dolls in the garage, telling me, "That's the old me … I'm over all that now." Dr. Ben was busier than ever operating on the increasing number of boys sent from the front in Vietnam. All of the information I could get about Eric came from him.

—They're preparing to court martial him, Karen. He'll have to go up before a military tribunal.

—What's going to happen to him?

—Hard to say. He resisted arrest and assaulted an officer.

—What about the drug charge? Isn't that really serious?

—It would be. But they've dropped it. They found marijuana in Frank Houseman's room. And the driver of the jeep apparently made a statement that he had provoked Eric by using racist language. This will stand Eric in good stead when he goes before the tribunal. It was a natural thing to do, I mean, punch that guy, MP or no MP.

—So, what does it mean in the end?

—I don't know. Probably eighteen months to two years, depending on how good his lawyer is. He was about to desert to the Soviet Union. He was doing something very cowardly by the standards of any country's army. By the way, I've talked to the dean about you.

—Oh.

—They'll record that you had to withdraw for health reasons. This will mean that there will be no blot on your academic record. They could have failed you in all your courses.

He hugged me tightly, but I just fell limp in his arms.

I received a letter yesterday. It's from New Jersey. I won't bore you with all of it, daddy, but he did write this …

I am so grateful for everything you did for my son, Eric. If something had happened to him I would be all alone. You saved him, Karen. My son is deeply in love with you. I pray that you will be protected and that someday I will have the chance to meet you, hopefully together with Eric.
Sincerely,
Melvin Smith

Eric and I exchanged letters too. We wrote to each other every day. We talked mostly about the future, daddy, our future. You see, I have more than one reason to wait for him besides love, as if that wasn't enough.

I'm taking your hand in mine and putting it against my blueberry dress, daddy. It's the same cotton print dress that you gave me when I turned sixteen. I'm the same person as I was then and I can still fit into it, daddy, though only barely now. Here, feel my belly. Can you feel it? In a few months' time I'm going to have Eric's baby. I'm placing your palm flat against my belly, daddy. Feel it. Can you feel it? Your grandchild is in there. Your angel is going to give birth to a baby.

The door is opening. I twist my neck around and see Dr. Cohen in his handsome three-piece suit. He's followed by Chuck Price, the little green intern. But I'm still holding your palm against my belly. I'm not letting go yet. I want them to see us like this. This is me, daddy, your own daughter, Karen. Me, connected to you.

Dr. Cohen is examining you while the intern stands over me.

—I'm afraid that your father has expired, Miss Rogers. When did he stop breathing? Did you notice?

The intern put his hand on the back of my chair. He frowned as he spoke to the doctor.

—She must have dozed off. I told her to press the button, but she must have dozed off. When I came in in the middle of the night she was fast asleep. Some girls just don't care whether their fathers live or die.

I wasn't asleep, daddy, but only you know that. So long as you know it, I can live with anything, even lies. There is no fog anywhere now, daddy, not around me.

I'm putting your hand back on the bed. There, it's resting against your side, peacefully. Goodbye, daddy. I know that you heard everything and, who knows, maybe you even understood everything too.

I'm standing up now, with my palm on my belly. I'm smiling at the two men by your bed. And I'm looking down on you.

I'm definitely smiling … and I'm on my way home.